Life's A Piece of Cake

D. LaShawn

ISBN: 978-0-9987207-0-8

Life's A Piece of Cake is a work of fiction. All characters and places appearing in this work are fictitious. Any resemblance to real persons, living or dead, places, establishments, events, organizations, and/or locations is purely coincidental and a product of the author's mind.

First Printing, 2017

*To my grandma, Grape, you loving me and me
loving you was a pure dee-light.*

———————————

ACKNOWLEDGEMENTS

I love and appreciate my family and those close to me, I'm certain if I started naming names, I'd be sure to forget someone and I don't want that to happen. Therefore, to each and everyone connected to me that had anything to do with helping this book to be published, I acknowledge and thank you.

To those who have been for me and to those who haven't been for me, I too, acknowledge you. For without you, whichever side you may find yourself on, I would not be where I am today. Therefore, truly from my heart to yours, I say thank you!

To my circle, my team, my family and friends, I'm eternally grateful for each of you. God blessing me with all of you in my life is a debt I'll never be able to repay.

If you are holding this book in your hands and reading these words, then I also acknowledge and thank you as well, I'm grateful you'd take the time to read words I've written. It truly means a lot to me.

Prologue

"So that was easy as pie." Erica said.

"You know, it kills me when people say things like that, easy as pie or life's a piece a cake. They apparently don't know what it takes to make a pie or bake a cake." Deidra said laughing.

Using sarcasm, Erica smiled saying, "Only a baker would ruin a such good cliché as those."

Two officers walked into King's Bakery, Deidra's very first bakery.

"Is Deidra King here?"

"How may I help you gentlemen?" Deidra asked.

"Ma'am, are you Deidra King?"

The hairs on the back of Deidra's neck began to rise up, her skin began to feel prickly. Her tongue immediately became coated with an unfamiliar taste.

Slow to answer, Deidra squinted and replied, "Yes, I'm Deidra King."

"Ma'am can you step from behind the counter?"

Thanking God the bakery was empty at the time and the children were still at school, Deidra removed her apron and walked from behind the counter towards the officers.

"Deidra King, you are under arrest. You have the right to remain silent. Anything you say can and will be used against you in a court of law. You have the right to speak to an attorney and to have an attorney present during any questioning." The officers recited.

Looking back at Erica, Deidra gave her "the nod," Erica knew exactly what everyone of Deidra's unspoken words meant.

Chapter 1

"Is this for real? I feel like it is but I'm pretty sure I don't know what is going on in my life right now. I seriously can't believe what is happening. I guess now for the first time I can join the ranks of those who've had out of body experiences because right now, that's how I feel. I'm walking but I'm not sure how. I can hear but I'm not sure how. I can see everything in front of me but again, I'm not quite sure how. It's weird, I know I have on an orange jump suit but only because the lady in the in-take room told me because when I see it, it looks grey just like everything else. It seems that now my mind has exchanged my ability to see in color to seeing everything in shades of grey."

Standing in front of the locked bars, the correctional officer, Officer Hardy smirked and said, "Welcome," before removing the clanking key ring from her holster. Opening the bars, Officer Hardy yelled out, "Hey, you, Maxine, wake up and welcome your new roommate."

A mixture of cold and heat rose up within Deidra King as she screamed out in her head, *"Roommate, I don't plan on staying here. Is she crazy?"*

Deidra's thoughts had her locked, fears of crossing that threshold rendered her weak, she couldn't move. Never in a million years had she ever imagined, she would be here, in this moment, at this place, in this particular time in life. No, not me, not Deidra Renee King, it just isn't possible.

Officer Hardy snapped, "Hey move it, what are you waiting for, a red carpet? If you are, you ain't getting it in here, get inside."

With a slight push to Deidra's back, Officer Hardy made sure she crossed the threshold to her jail cell. Those big, black bars slid shut so fast Deidra felt hypnotized, she was now officially behind bars.

"I can see you've never been here before," Maxine said laughing as she eased down from the top bed.

Calling it a bed is a far cry from the truth, nothing like the beds in real homes but that's what it looked like.

Deidra's feet felt as if they were in cement blocks, not that there was much room to walk to begin with but she had a hard time even moving her feet to go to her…bed.

"I've been around long enough to know when someone doesn't belong in here and missy, you are one of them. What are you in here for?"

Making it to her side of the room, Deidra rubbed her temples in an effort to remove some of the tension in her head, she whispered, "I'd rather not talk about it."

Taking real slow steps towards her new roommate, Maxine said, "Oh, so not only do you not belong in here but you think you're better than us that are?"

"Maxine is it? Listen, I never said that. I really would just like to be left alone, this hasn't been the easiest day for me, okay. I'm not here to make friends and I don't plan on being here very long, I'm sure my bail will be posted soon." Deidra explained.

Laughing hysterically, Maxine slapped her knee while grabbing her stomach.

"What's so funny?" Deidra asked.

"Oh this ain't T.V. Miss Thing, this is the real deal. You do realize you can't get bail without an arraignment hearing and it is Friday night." Maxine said laughing.

"So. What does that have to do with me?" Deidra replied.

"Oh honey, boy do you have a lot to learn. The judge here doesn't arraign on the weekends, he won't be here until Monday morning, which means, you will be here until then."

Running towards the bars, Deidra grabbed them and yelled out, "Oh no, I can't stay here until Monday morning, my friend is supposed to be posting my bail tonight. I need to get out of here."

"Uh yeah, about that. Ain't going to happen, you may as well get that in your head now. You may as well stop all that hollering and dramatics on those bars, nobody cares or is even listening to you and to be frank, I don't want to hear it. The sooner you realize you are in jail, the better off you'll be. You, my friend, are locked up. Uh-huh, I bet you want to talk now huh?"

Beginning to understand Maxine's point as no one came to check, slowly, Deidra turned around. Walking back to her side of the cell, she stood in the corner with her arms folded across her chest.

"So what are you in for?" Deidra asked.

Waving a finger, Maxine said, "No, no, no, I asked you first. But seeing as you are scared out of your mind. I'll be glad to go first."

Making herself comfortable on Deidra's bed, Maxine said, "Well, for me, I'm back home. I was released from prison about three months ago but hey, I quickly learned, there isn't anything for me out there. In here, I get three meals a day, clothes on my back, and I'm sheltered. I don't have to live on the streets, like I did before. So I committed armed robbery for the fifteenth time in my life. Now, I'm waiting for my sentencing hearing, I'm waiting to see where they are going to send me this time."

Exhibiting a sense of accomplishment and air of pride, Maxine smiled and looked over at me as I stood in astonishment.

"You can't be serious? Fifteen times? Are you trying to tell me you'd rather be locked up like a caged animal than out there living life as a free person?" Deidra asked.

"Does living out there guarantee you freedom? Do you really believe that? I was made to believe growing up as a child that life's a piece of cake, as my grandmother used to say, she used to say, life is easy, life is sweet, like a piece of cake. That's a lie. Life is mean and it's hard. The truth is, nothing about my life was ever sweet or easy. Even when I've been free as you call it, I've felt locked up and caged in. They say life's a piece of cake but no one ever tells you that cake might be poisonous."

Listening to Maxine, Deidra looked over at her as she spoke. Watching her as the words came from her mouth, she felt like she was looking at a shell of a woman but also in a strange way, she felt like she was also looking in a mirror.

To hear Maxine talk, she sounded as if life had robbed her of any hope in life. To look at her, one could tell life had hardened her. The lines in her face and the greying of her hair was evidence to her aging but not gracefully.

Attending to the words she spoke, Deidra saw somewhat of herself in what she was sharing.

Squinting her eyes to focus on Maxine, Deidra realized, she too had taken on a façade of a sweet, little life. A life she'd created to cover up and conceal all that had happened in her childhood as well as even now. Like, Maxine, her life was anything but sweet and tasty like cake, in fact, it was very bitter and nasty.

Chapter 2

"So what's your name doll?" Maxine inquired.

Having heard Maxine talk a little, she decided to let her guard down somewhat and said, "Deidra. Deidra King."

Jumping off Deidra's bed, Maxine shouted, "King, you said? Man, that reminds me, I almost robbed this bakery not too far from here called King's Bakery. I cased that joint for a while but at the last minute, something kept me from hitting them up."

Tapping her foot, with crossed arms, Deidra said, "Well, I don't know if I should thank you or smack you. Had you robbed that place, you would have been robbing me. That's one of the several bakeries I happen to own."

Maxine's hand flew to her mouth, "Get out of town, are you pulling my leg?"

"No, I'm not, one of my stores is only a few miles from here, over on MLK Boulevard, is that the one you were eyeing?" Deidra asked.

"What a small freaking world." Maxine said loudly. "I'm sorry little mama, no disrespect to you. You have a nice shop, good stuff in there too. The samples were great. Listen to me, I'm telling you, something kept me from going there. You must have some serious prayers going up for you or something."

Scratching her salt and peppered afro, Maxine asked, "So, if you own several bakeries, I really want to know now, how did you end up in here? I could tell from the moment I saw you that you didn't belong in here but why are you here?"

"It's a long story." Deidra said.

"We got all weekend." Maxine said smiling.

Hearing Maxine, Deidra didn't know if she wanted to laugh or cry. They both laughed at her stating the obvious.

Since Maxine was on Deidra's bed, she hopped up to hers. As Deidra's feet swung back and forth, she said, "I'm not sure how I ended up here. Right now, everything is a blur to me…my life right now is a blur."

"Well, let's see, let's start from the beginning." Maxine suggested. "Are your parents still together?"

Deidra laughed so hard, she almost peed in her jumpsuit, the orange one that still looked gray.

"When did asking about parents become comedy central?" Maxine wondered aloud.

Getting herself together, she explained, "No, no, no, you don't understand. I'm laughing because my parents were never together so to hear a question like that cracked me up. When I was born, my parents were kids, they weren't parents. My mother was a Freshman in High School when she had me and my father, let me rephrase that, my donor, didn't even graduate from High School. He was a slightly older guy who got my mother pregnant and left her to figure things out on her own. He was quite clear about not wanting to be involved in my life. I only saw him on a few occasions and I wish I could forget those times I did see him."

"I grew up without a father either but why do you say you wish you could forget ever seeing him? I think, even to this day, I would give anything just to have one conversation with my father. I mean, I think I'd try to be nice but I think I'd really want to ask him why he never came for me? Why he never wanted to take me to the park and push me on the swings or tell me I was beautiful. I think if given the chance I'd want to ask him those things. I'm fifty years old and I still have those questions." Maxine shared.

Feeling the burn in the back of her eyes, Deidra wanted to know the same things, she had those same questions. He was supposed to be the one man in my life that would love me unconditionally and keep me protected and make me feel safe and all he ever did was make me feel ugly and insecure.

Deidra's feet stopped swinging and said, "I remember this one day, my mom dressed me up in my best Easter dress and took me to see him. I was so happy, my grandmother swooned over me before we left telling me how pretty I was. She patted my long beautiful locks, my mother had spent all morning doing my hair for my visit. My grandmother raised me since my mother was so young and a teen mom without any assistance my father and she kept telling me how pretty I looked in my dress."

The pain of the memory started to manifest as Deidra talked with Maxine and her voice hitched a bit but she pushed past it.

"When we arrived, I couldn't wait to show my dad how I looked. When I saw him, I can remember asking, "Daddy, do you like my dress and my hair?"

There was no more holding back the tears, they decided to go against her will and they began to flow, Deidra followed through and told Maxine the rest of the story by saying, "Do you know that man, in his raggedy, run down one room apartment had the nerve to say to a child, his child, "No, I don't, you look ugly. You look nothing like me. You're not my daughter."

Maxine jumped up from my bed with her fists balled up, air boxing saying, "Oh, where is he? Let me at him, I want to teach him a lesson."

Smiling through her tears at Maxine Deidra said, "I don't even think his words hit me as hard as the push out the door from my mother. Man, she pushed me so hard and fast out that door and I remember I ran and ran until I found myself underneath a creepy stairwell under his room where I heard screaming and cursing. I was so hurt, I was afraid, I was lonely, I couldn't understand how he could be so cruel to me, to his daughter. The next thing I knew a hand snatched me from under that stairwell. My mother grabbed me and when we left my dad's place that day, we never looked back."

"I'm sorry to hear that girlfriend, I can't even imagine, now I understand why you wish you could forget. Well, it sounds like your mom wasn't having none of that. She sounded like she did what she could to protect you."

Deidra's feet began to swing a little. She looked up at the ceiling and with a big sigh, replied, "Yeah, I guess. She did the best she could. She and my grandmother. But you know what, sometimes your best still isn't good enough," as her voice trailed off.

"What do you mean by that Deidra?" Maxine asked.

Deidra's eyes led her towards the ceiling. She couldn't understand why but she was fixated on what she saw above. The cracks in the ceiling worried her. There were a lot of them. She started to think the ceiling could fall on her at any moment. She had never shared with anyone about things in her past and now she was baring her soul to a complete stranger who so happened to be her cellmate.

Well, with nothing to lose, she said, "Well, when my mother graduated from High School, she immediately went into the military, she did it to provide a better life for us and she granted custody to my grandmother during her time of service. Just so you see the pattern here, my grandmother wasn't married, she was a single mom, who had my mom, who wasn't married and became a single mom. Got it, you see the pattern?" I asked.

"Yep, got it and yes, I see it." Maxine shouted.

"Despite my grandmother being an amazing woman, she did a horrible job picking men. Unfortunately, I watched her suffer from such heartache and pain from one failed relationship to the other. The men would come and the next thing I know, they'd be gone. Just like that. Which for me, shaped my foundational views on relationships."

"Yeah, I could see that." Maxine chimed in.

Running her hands through her hair, Deidra said, "There was this one guy in particular, when I was about six years old, he changed the course of my life FOREVER."

Engaged in Deidra's story, Maxine leaned in and said, "What happened Deidra?"

"I can still remember like it was yesterday, he came into my bedroom while I was asleep. He reeked of old cigarettes, whatever beer old men drink, and the same for his cologne, whatever old men thought they smelled good in but didn't. Either singularly or as a combination, those smells are forever burned into my nostrils. They now serve as massive triggers for me, I try to avoid them at all costs. He was a vile and disgusting man. I can't believe I'm saying this now but that man molested me." She confessed as her hands began to tremble.

Jumping up again, air boxing, Maxine shouted again, "Oh let me at him. I would like to get a piece of him."

Shaking her head at Maxine, she continued on, "You are the only person I've ever told this to. Do you realize I haven't been able to tell anyone this, not my mother and certainly not my grandmother. I mean, to be honest, I wasn't quite sure what had even happened to me. What was I to say?"

Hopping down to the floor, Deidra's emotions began to take over, she was now more animated than ever. she looked right at Maxine and declared, "I didn't know then but I definitely know now. Maxine, not only did he sexually abuse me but he stole my innocence, my youth, my hope, my dreams. What kind of a sick…oops, I almost said a bad word and I quit doing that years ago."

Maxine jumped up air boxing again and proudly stated, "Well, I haven't." For about two minutes straight Maxine called Deidra's grandmother's boyfriend every name in the book and some she even made up because some Deidra had never in life heard of some of those words.

Settling back down. Deidra let Maxine in on another secret, she said, "It was from that moment that because I couldn't control what was happening in my life, I decided to control what I could. I had to pretend nothing had happened, right? I had to pretend I wasn't hurting; I essentially grew up pretending so I began to create an alternate world for me to live in. One that would appear as if everything around me was easy, that nothing could touch me, that in my mind, life would become what I wanted it to be, like a piece of cake."

Chapter 3

"Speaking of cake; I sure could use a piece right now, my stomach just revealed to me, I'm starving."

Deidra's stomach was touching her back by this point and she hadn't noticed until the noises her stomach was making sounded like there were three of them conversing in that cell.

Rubbing her stomach, she said, "I haven't eaten all day. With everything that has happened today, I'm guessing that it's probably close to midnight by now, right?"

Pointing to a small clock hanging on the wall in the guard's station off in the distance, Maxine said, "I hope you have sonar vision because even with my 20/20, it's hard to see the time but I think you're right, it looks like midnight. Can I offer you a bologna sandwich my lady?" In her best Italian voice, she said, "It's imported straight from Italy."

Repulsed at the thought, Deidra gagged a little. The thought of eating a bologna sandwich took her back to the days she lived in the projects. She'd worked her tail off to live a life so different from that. She hadn't eaten a bologna sandwich in years and she didn't want to start today.

Observant of her internal conflict, Maxine chuckled and said, "Oh well, I guess you ain't too hungry, huh girlfriend?"

Little did she know, Deidra's stomach begged to differ. After wrestling with her pride, with reluctance, Deidra took the sandwich and thanked her.

Slowly unwrapping the sandwich, Maxine snatched the sandwich from me and said, "Girl, give it to me."

Stashed away in a corner of the cell, Maxine pulled out a brown bag filled to the brim with all sort of things. It was unbelievable. She began to work like a mad scientist in a lab. Maxine pulled out an unknown bag of chips, called, Shabang. Opening up the sandwich, she crushed the chips over the meat and carefully spread mustard and mayo on the slices of bread. Handing over a plate, she placed the newly improved sandwich and a honey bun on the side, along with a bag of Tang powered juice.

"Wow, Chef Maxine, what a meal we have here." Deidra said looking in awe.

"I'll have some noodles for us tomorrow, that's the real treat," Maxine said with assurance. "But I need to get to the shower water first since that's the only hot water we have access to." She explained.

Judging from the look on Deidra's confused face, Maxine laughed and said, "Don't worry, I'll show you tomorrow, how we cook around here."

It was refreshing to Deidra to for Maxine to realize she would need to break things down for her, she was grateful for her.

"Oh my goodness, are you sure I'm not eating steak and shrimp? Maxine, this is the best bologna, shabang sandwich I've ever eating." Deidra exclaimed.

In total, Deidra drank four cups of Tang that night. She didn't even mind the water came from a faucet that was connected to the toilet. Shoot, who was she kidding, right then and there, that toilet water tasted good.

Laughing hysterically, Maxine said, "Not bad huh? Now you know what it's like to be real hungry."

Deidra couldn't help but laugh, saying, "You are so right but Maxine, how did you make that food taste like a five-star meal? Anyone who can do what you just did, has real talent or I was just real hungry. Either way, I'm very impressed."

Rubbing her now full belly, she wondered, "*How can she get used to this? This isn't any way to live. I ate that because I had to but she eats it because she wants to. I'm here because I have to be, she comes here because she wants to. I know one thing, when I get out of this mess, I'm never coming back here.*"

Smiling, Maxine said, "Well, you know, when I was a little girl, I wanted to be a chef, I had dreams of making people happy with my food. I've always enjoyed seeing people light up when they taste my food. I've been cooking for a long time, I had to grow up fast and I learned how to always make something out of nothing."

Watching Maxine talk about her childhood dreams, Deidra felt connected to her story. She had indeed made her happy with her food and she could only imagine what she'd do with quality ingredients. While she lit up talking about her aspirations, Deidra could still see an emptiness within her.

Yet, something about her eyes comforted Deidra and in a way, she reminded her of her deceased grandmother, the same way her eyes would comfort her when I needed it.

In the time she'd been in the cell with Maxine, she'd done most of the talking but as Deidra devoured her food, Maxine's conversation about herself picked up.

Maxine talked about her children that she never knew. About how she too was raised by an elderly woman to whom she looked at as a grandmother figure.

"Grape is what we called her," Maxine said. "She took in my twin brother and me, when I was born. Like you, I was also a product of a teen mom. Rumor has it, she was about twelve years old and gave birth to twins. Her mother forced her to give the kids up for adoption. The lady who raised us was a nurse at the hospital and agreed to adopt us. She died when we were about fifteen and everything in my life changed when she died."

Vulnerability was all over Maxine, she was opening up as she fought back the tears.

Deidra found herself starting to enjoy her company and conversations.

In that moment, Deidra vowed to herself to take care of Maxine. She decided that when she got out the next time, she would take her in and provide her with a job and a place to stay in order to get her established. Deidra wanted to give her a reason to live and accomplish her dreams. Even if she didn't want it, Deidra wanted her to do better and be better. She wanted her to see another side of life and show her that faith and fear can't reside in the same dwelling. Strangely enough, Deidra now felt responsible for Maxine.

As she pondered her decision, Deidra wondered, *"Maybe the reason, bad things are happening to me is because I'm the good thing needed to happen to someone else."*

Unable and unwilling to focus on her own thoughts at the moment, not at a time when Maxine was opening up about her life. Deidra realized, she had to listen, she wanted to listen, she needed to listen.

"My brother and I ended up in foster care after her death. The only problem was, we were separated and sent to different homes. I mean, who does that? Who splits up siblings?" Maxine shouted.

Unsure of how to respond, Deidra only nodded in agreement with her and continued to listen.

"After being raped repeatedly, beaten repeatedly, I was then introduced to drugs, I welcomed anything that could take away my pain." Maxine explained.

Walking over to the corner of the cell, Maxine stood with folded arms across her chest saying, "I have no idea where my brother is, I tried keeping in touch with him but we lost contact after the first set of foster parents. They really need to do better screenings with these people who want to become foster parents."

Shaking her head, still unable to offer much, Deidra simply said, "I can't even imagine."

"When most kids are celebrating their "Sweet Sixteen" birthdays, I was already a High School dropout, strung out on drugs, and homeless. The streets became my new home. That last foster family did it for me, I felt like the streets as unfriendly as they were would be more kind to me. Sad huh?" Maxine said.

The weight of Maxine's story landed on Deidra's shoulders and also in her heart, her heart ached for her. However, the revelations of her past allowed Deidra to understand why she didn't mind being locked up. In a weird way, it made sense.

"Maxine, how many children do you have?"

"I have two kids out there somewhere. I survived the streets by prostituting myself. I lived on drugs and alcohol…not the healthiest of diets. As a result, I was out of my mind. I left one of my children on the doorstep of a really, nice two-story home with a well-manicured lawn and a playground. And my other one, I'm not sure what happened to her, I had her in an alley. I wrapped her up in newspaper and found the nearest hospital. I left her by the front door and ran away." Maxine confessed.

Maxine's confession scorched Deidra's ears. Thinking she was doing a good job of managing her facial expressions with the emotional toll of Maxine's stories but she was proven wrong when Maxine snapped, "Don't judge me because I sin differently than you do, Miss Thing."

Jumping up to rush by Maxine's side and speaking with rushed words, Deidra said, "Oh no, no, no, it's not that at all, trust me, I have no room to judge you Maxine. In fact, God is still working on me. Too many times, I've seen where others are quick to pass judgment on you instead of looking at themselves. Who am I to look down on you because of your situation, in the blink of an eye, things can change in a wrong direction, real bad and real quick for any of us."

Noticing one solitaire tear dropping from Maxine's face, Deidra said, "No judgement, just a hug. Can I give you a hug right now?"

Extending her arms towards Deidra, she walked closer for their embrace, an embrace that felt nurturing like a mother does to her child. Deidra knew she wanted to offer support to Maxine in the hug but deep down, she felt needed it too. Whispering in her ears, before breaking loose, Deidra said, "Everything will be okay, you are going to make it."

Both Maxine and Deidra shared matching tears, they each had a few tears to fall.

Remembering she had to be tough, Maxine pulled back and blurted, "I'm a survivor, not a victim. Don't cry about my situation if I ain't crying. Besides, karma has done a number on me over the years. That's why my life took the turn that it took. I've hated myself for many years, but I know my kids had a better chance at life if they were far away from me." Maxine laughed and sighed as she said, "Karma…when a bird is alive, it eats ants. When a bird dies, ants eat it."

As strangely as it sounded at that moment, Deidra totally understood what she meant.

"I once heard someone say, "We have two lives, the one we learn with and the one we live with after that," said Maxine.

"Life is what you make it." Deidra chimed in.

"Yeah, I guess you're right." Maxine replied.

Feeling a sense to go deeper, Deidra could feel a source of energy, she wasn't familiar with but she submitted to it. Taking in a deep breath she said, "Maxine, unfortunately, people only see the choices we make, never do they see the options from which we had to choose. You made the choices you had to make in life and I'm sorry you went through that pain. But listen, he who dwells on the past, robs the present; but he who ignores the past, robs the future. Your past is a part of you, embrace it. Learn from it. Remember, if you do what you always did, you will get what you always got."

Nodding her head, Maxine replied, "Yeah, that's deep."

Chapter 4

"Hey, you better try to get some sleep. Before you know it, it'll be time for roll call, then breakfast." Maxine explained.

"Yeah, I think you're right, it's been a long day." Deidra answered.

"Goodnight Deidra." Maxine said softly.

"Goodnight Maxine."

It is unimaginable for anyone to understand how cold it was in the dark cell even if you've been in some pretty cold climates, it was ten times colder than that. However, it wasn't just the temperature that chilled the air but the environment alone was cold and dark. The blanket they provided, if you can even call it that was torn and raggedy. It lacked the warmth and coziness the regular blankets produced.

The cracks in the ceiling caught Deidra's eye once again. Focusing in on them, the chilly air didn't bother her as much. Caught up in the thoughts swirling in her head, she wondered, "*Why do I keep finding the cracks in the ceiling? Do they represent the cracks in my life? How did I end up here? Did I crack under the pressure? Will I crack under this pressure?*"

Maxine's snores allowed Deidra to drown out the other unpleasant sounds surrounding me. She knew within minutes; sleep wasn't in her future.

"Wake up Princesses. Roll Call." Officer Hardy shouted.

The personal 2:00 a.m. wake up call was accompanied by guards banging on the bars of the cells.

"*Seriously?*" Deidra thought.

The process to scan the wristband barcodes of each inmate was intense, Deidra thought as she sat back and observed, "*I have never in my life witnessed such an exercise. I'm outside of my element and I'm completely fine with that. This isn't anything I want to get used to.*"

"Oops, my bad…I forget to tell you about that. I hope it didn't scare you too much." Maxine said laughing.

Lying back down, Deidra replied, "I'm alright."

Able to finally close her eyes, Deidra thought she was dreaming when the lights came on again and she heard, "Breakfast, line up." This announcement was courtesy of the 4:00 a.m. wake up call.

Not having been in a single file line since elementary school days - field trips, Deidra now found herself in one to receive her breakfast tray. At least, she thought it was breakfast, it was supposed to be breakfast.

She forced myself to eat what appeared to be grits, a sausage patty, and a biscuit and gravy.

Luckily, she was able to go back to her cell and sleep. Can you believe it, she was able to sleep for more than two hours and for the first time in twenty-four hours, she felt at peace.

"What are you smiling for Sunshine?" Maxine asked as she walked in our cell with an older inmate.

"Oh well, you know, God woke me up this morning. In a bed, per se and not in a casket. Everyday above ground is a good day, right? That's reason enough to smile, do you think?" Deidra said.

Had Deidra known what would happen next, she more than likely would not have asked that particular question. As a result, an avalanche of scornful questions and concerns were unleashed on her.

"If there really was a God, why did He let us end up here? Why has the devil gotten ahold of us and won't let go? My mother was a prayer warrior but why did God let her die of cancer? Why has He continuously tested my faith all of these years? Yeah, I stopped praying long ago. It may work for some, but, people like me don't get their prayers answered. This is an evil world we live in, shawty. You feel me?"

Listening to this woman, Deidra's thoughts raced, *"Whoa, remind me who I say that too next time. I didn't expect all of that to come from this lady. But now that is has, Lord, how do I respond? I'm not trying to make any enemies here; I need to respond with love to this woman. I've learned... Love is the only force capable of transforming an enemy into a friend."*

Carefully choosing her words and with a warm smile, Deidra replied, "Ms...I apologize, I didn't catch your name."

"Just call me Shank," replied the older woman without hesitation.

"I'm scared to know why her name is Shank," Deidra thought to herself as she pretended to be unphased by the name.

Extending her hand, she said, "Nice to meet you Shank. You know what, once upon a time, I would have agreed with you. I too, over the years, questioned my faith. But over time, I learned that evil can be a good thing. The evil things in this life are necessary and are designed to bring us closer to God. You know, sometimes, it's not always the Devil. God orchestrate things to happen a certain way to direct us to Him."

Shank didn't appear to be taking in Deidra's words of encouragement but she was undeterred, she continued on. "You see; I remember the day I prayed for the things I have now. God may have let you stay in a bad spot or with your back against the wall, just to eventually show you how great and powerful He really is. He gives the necessary life experiences in order to wake you up. He may be holding you back temporarily until the road ahead is safe and clear to continue. When you realize that, you become thankful for that stall."

"How old are you youngster?" Shank snarled.

"I'll be thirty on my next birthday." Deidra replied.

Shank laughed and said, "Thirty, you're still a baby. Looking at you, I wouldn't put you a day over twenty, you still have a lot of growing and maturing to do, but you are wise beyond your years. I like the way you think young grasshopper."

Shaking her head and laughing, Deidra said, "Trust me, I don't look like what I've been through, I'll tell you that. Maturity comes with experiences, not age."

"And there she goes again, my girl is straight up wise around here. That little bit of sleep you got, got you spitting out all kinds of wisdom this morning" Maxine shouted.

"Struggle, pain, and failure have all been my experiences," Shank confessed.

"It is the struggle that makes accomplishments more meaningful." Deidra affirmed her.

Kneeling down beside her, Deidra said, "Listen to me Shank, pain is simply the result of the failure to acknowledge something that is staring you right in the face. And not only that but failure is necessary to appreciate success."

It was apparent these women had some really hard knock lives. Totally different from the reserved, sheltered life, Deidra had come to know, the once she'd created.

"You know what, I'm going to pray for strength and guidance for you ladies." Deidra offered.

"No. I don't need you to pray for me no strength because I may take it and beat somebody to death." Shank responded

Everyone looked at each other and erupted with laughter, somehow, Maxine and Deidra felt Shank was partly joking and partly serious.

Standing to leave, Shank turned to Deidra and said, "I heard you young grasshopper, I want you to know, I got mad respect for you, keep doing what you doing. You talking like that, the way you just talked to me. Whatever you in here for, it won't matter and it won't stick. If for nothing else, you were sent here for me."

With a pounded fist to her chest, Shank walked away saying, "One love…I'll get up with y'all later."

Sitting on the bed, processing Shank's words, Deidra's heart and head swirled. All she could think was, *"Wow, that was powerful but if she only knew what I've done."*

"Hey, you got any kids?" Maxine asked.

"Yes, I have two. A nine year old daughter and a one year old son."

"I'm sure that big gap in their ages wasn't planned, huh girlfriend?" Maxine asked.

"Not at all." Denise chuckled.

"My daughter was a product of my wild college days. I was still kind of young myself and didn't know the first thing about having a baby. I made my bed, literally, and I made the decision to lie in it. Having her changed my life forever. God chose me to be her mother. He sent her to me to save me from myself. That's a debt I'll never be able to repay." Deidra explained.

Talking about her children pricked her heart, talking about them forced Deidra to wonder how they were doing and if they were questioning where she was. She was sure her daughter was old enough to wonder.

Looking over at Maxine, to keep from crying, Deidra said, "Running away from any problem only increases the distance from the solution. The easiest way to escape from the problem is to solve it. So you know what, I put on my big girl panties and accepted my responsibilities, even knowing I would be doing it alone."

Standing up from her bed, Deidra turned around and said, "The day she was born, I remember looking into her eyes and thinking…to the world you may be one person. But to one person, you may be the world. I was her world. She depended on me. I had to drop out of school for about a year or so, until I was able to get back on my feet and finish what I started."

Maxine chimed in, "Anyone can start strong but everyone won't finish strong. Always finish what you start. I can hear my grandmother's voice ringing in my ears as she would constantly say that to me and my brother."

"Your grandmother sounds like she was a very wise woman and you know what, I did finish what I started. I went back to school and received my Bachelors in Computer Engineering and Business Management."

Interrupting Deidra, Maxine said, "I knew you were some 'ole smart nerd."

Deidra laughed and said, "Maxine, you are hilarious."

"You laughing and I'm so serious…I knew it when I saw you, I thought, nerd alert."

"Maxine, you are too funny. In all seriousness though, for years, I tried my best to be the best example to my daughter. I wanted to show her how strong a woman can be. All I want is for one day, my kids to remember their childhood and say their mother gave it her best. She wasn't perfect and failed sometimes but she always got back up and tried again. I want them to say I taught them honesty, kindness, hard work, morals, respect, integrity, love, making right decisions, even if she had to learn from her own mistakes, but that I loved them enough to keep trying. I want them to remember that when life knocked me down… I ALWAYS got back up. I want my kids to be able to say, I'm proud of you mom and because of you, I didn't give up. It took me a little while to actually realize that children hear everything you say and mimic all you do. I had to make sure to give them a good example. I know that when I finish raising them, the world has to deal with them. I just hope I'm doing a great job with them before I send them off to live life in this crazy harsh world."

Chapter 5

"Sounds like you're a great mom but -ter-uh, Deidra, I'm trying to understand how someone goes from having college degrees, to living their dreams, owning successful bakeries, to wearing orange jumpsuits, sharing a cell with me, and moonlight preaching to other inmates. Can you explain that to me? I need to know what happened to you girlfriend." Maxine inquired with her arms folded and a confused look on her face.

"Life happened Maxine. Life, that's what happened." Deidra responded holding her head down in shame.

Maxine walked over to Deidra, placing her hand under her chin and said, "Hold your head up Queen, your crown is falling."

Those words, they transported Deidra to a time back in her life, they pierced through her like a sword, she couldn't identify the feelings but she snapped out of my shame, jerking her head back and said, "Wait, what did you just say to me?

Before she could repeat it, Deidra said, "I remember hearing those same words when I was very young riding around with my granny."

Standing in the middle of the jail cell, Deidra's mind took her back to when she was a little girl, she stood frozen, as if she was suspended in time travel, she began to recount the memories.

"I recognize the house." she said, remembering.

"You're starting to freak me out a little bit girlfriend, what house are you supposedly seeing?" Maxine asked.

"No, shh, listen, it's all coming back to me. My granny and I had ridden by this house so many times. I know she thought I was asleep but you know what they say, all eyes closed ain't sleep. Anyway, my granny pulled up to this yellow and white house, she ran two small boxes, wrapped in red Christmas paper and an envelope to the mailbox. As she turned to run back to the car, an older lady came to the door."

Deidra's throat was getting dry, the memories were rushing to her quicker than she could process them, she stopped for a drink of water.

Ccontinuing on, "The older lady said, you've been doing this for years and this is the first time I've been able to catch you. Usually you send it through the mail with no return address or drop it by in the wee hours of the night. I knew one of these days, I'd catch up with you. My grandmother leaned in and said to the lady, how are they? Are they having a good birthday? I heard the lady ask my grandma, you want to meet them? They know they are adopted. My granny slowly started walking away, she said, no, I think it'll be too much, I was only dropping off something for them."

Deidra's voice started to hitch as she pushed through the story, the recollections were intense and taking an emotional toll.

Deidra sat down and said, "I remember the old lady walking down the steps towards my granny and saying, "I wanted to contact you but your mother felt very strongly about you having kids at such a young age. As the years went on, I thought you had moved on with your life and I didn't want to disrupt anything for you. But I want you to know, they've had a good life here, they both are doing well. My granny thanked the lady for taking care of her children and began to cry. She shook her head and said, I don't want to ruin their birthday, this may be too much for them to handle today, I should probably go. I guess the lady understood because she obliged my granny but told her to hold on for a moment and went inside the house. She later came out with a photo album and handed it to my granny. As my grandmother took the book, and opened it, she began to hold her head down and sob uncontrollably. The old woman placed her head under her chin and said, "There, there now, hold your head up Queen, your crown is falling."

Maxine was now frozen, she looked at Deidra and said, "Now, I know you were young but do you know what day that birthday was on?"

"Yes, I do…if I remember correctly, I remember my grandma saying, "It's 12/22, their birthday, I'm only here to drop off something for them."

"Do you by chance know what gift she left?" Maxine asked.

"No, I don't…I don't remember that." Deidra said.

Maxine was in tears, she pulled out a picture from under her stash of belongings, a picture of her on her birthday wearing a heart-shaped necklace standing in front of a white and yellow house.

"Deidra, do you want to take a guess when my birthday is?"

"*No way,*" she thought to herself. "*Could it be? Could Maxine be my aun*t?

A secret's worth depends on the people from which it must be kept. Deidra's heart ached for Maxine not getting an opportunity to meet her mother, who could quite possibly be her grandmother, who was an awesome woman. Her heart ached for the life she ended up living as a result of not knowing she had family who would've loved and accepted her and her brother when their adopted mother died.

Deidra knew it was something about Maxine from the moment she saw her. Her eyes spoke to her, she felt like she'd seen them before. Truth is, she had, in her grandmother, her mother, hell, they were her eyes too. In looking at Maxine, she was essentially looking at herself.

For what felt like an eternity, they stood and embraced one another sobbing like crazy. In the last twelve hours, they'd been a source of encouragement and support for another and had shed some tears but this time, it was different. The bond they'd created earlier was now cemented by blood, without any DNA tests, they knew they were related.

"I'm going to help you get back on your feet and give you a reason to want to do and be better. Just look at this as your second chance." Deidra said to Maxine."

"I'm about on my eighth, second chance. I've done too many bad things. I don't deserve anything good to come of that. I've given up on a decent life on the outside." She replied.

"Oh no ma'am, I will not have you speaking that curse around me. I don't know where my story will end, but nowhere in my text will you ever read, that I gave up. For me, giving up is not an option, especially when I have two little people calling me mom and that should be your attitude too." Deidra said.

"Child, don't have all these high hopes for me. My world is over sweetheart." Maxine said accepting what seemed like her fate.

"Just when the caterpillar thought the world was over, she began to fly." Deidra reminded her.

"Well, Ms. Caterpillar, how much flying are you planning on doing when you still haven't told me what you're in here for?" Maxine said.

"I'm going to get to that." Deidra said laughing at her now crazy aunt.

"Well, before you tell me, I want you to know, I have so much respect for you Deidra. I love how you stay so strong, even when you have every reason to break down." Maxine said.

Holding Maxine's hand, she said, "In all my days, I've never met a strong person with an easy past. Sometimes you can't do anything but cry when you think back on all the things God has brought you through. I just refuse to cry over the same thing ever again once I cry about it. I'm a woman. Women are strong not because they never break, but because they know how to pick up the pieces and put themselves back together again. They know how to build a new foundation with the same bricks that were thrown at them. The same boiling water that softens the potato, hardens the egg. It's about what you're made of, not the circumstances."

"Well, will you look at God, my niece is my cellmate. I guess sometimes, our lives have to be completely shaken up, changed, and rearranged to put us in the place we were meant to be. I'm so sorry we met in the worst possible place on earth but baby girl, I'm so glad to have met you." Maxine said smiling.

Chapter 6

"Line up Buttercups… it's lunch time," a short haired officer yelled.

Maxine didn't budge.

Facing Maxine, Deidra asked, "Are you hungry?"

"Nah, not when it's the day they serve those horrible tasting pink hot dogs. Those things are hideous. I'd probably starve myself to death before I ever eat another one." Maxine replied.

Hard to contain the laughter, Deidra's laugh built up to a loud sounding one. Making a joke with Maxine, her new found aunt, Deidra jokingly said, "I'll take your word for it, hell, after being locked up fifteen times, I'd say, you're pretty credible when it comes to jailhouse food."

"Shoot, I'm more than credible, I'm prepared and resourceful…follow me girlfriend," Maxine said, reaching into her brown bag of stashed away goodies.

Happy to oblige Maxine, Deidra followed suit with a smile unsure of what Maxine had up her sleeve, literally.

Inside the women's showers, Maxine pulled out two cups of Noodles from her sleeve and handed me one of the cups, smiling as she turned the shower water to the hottest setting possible and filled her cup.

Following her lead, Deidra couldn't help but smile as she was being schooled on a new trick, cooking without a stove.

Back inside the cell, Maxine took out two really thick books, *Moby Dick* and the *Bible*.

Noticing Deidra scratching her head in utter confusion, Maxine chuckled and said, "Now, let me show you to really cook in here."

Watching Maxine was like watching an exhibit in a museum, she was masterful with her techniques and presentation.

Maxine placed each book on top of the Noodles cups for about ten minutes to take advantage of the steamy, hot, shower water. During the wait time, she pulled out a pack of squeezable cheese and put it in a small white, Styrofoam cup. At the same time, she broke off pieces of hot sausage and bit into a kosher dill pickle pouch and poured off some of the juice. Mixing everything together in the cup of Noodles, it was like voila, a jailhouse gourmet meal.

Squealing with amusement, Deidra asked, "Oh my God, what in the world is this concoction? Wow, this is actually pretty good."

"You sound surprised niecey." Maxine said.

"If you only knew, I nearly gagged at the sight of all of those ingredients you mixed together but you are like an artist of some sort, you are amazing. I've often heard that people eat with their eyes first but people like me, with not much of a choice, don't have that kind of luxury. At least I didn't today but thank God it was good." Deidra replied.

"Thanks for keeping my stomach from rebelling, it was starting to get a little restless for a moment but you came through and hooked us up in here today Auntie. I think I'm going to go and actually use the shower to wash my body instead of cook my food this time." Deidra said chuckling.

Heading towards the shower, Deidra stopped in a panic from all too familiar sounds…the sounds of abuse may come in different forms, those impacted never forget the sound.

"Yeah, you ugly, black bitch; I took your food. I slapped you and spit on you, now tell me, what are you going to do about it, heffa?" Deidra heard standing in the not so far distance.

It's amazing how bullying brings back memories, horrible and terrifying ones.

Watching from a close distance Deidra stood thinking back to an unpleasant time in her life, a moment in time dating back to when she was a small girl in the second grade, a time she'd never forgotten.

Standing on the elementary school playground, Deidra remembered feeling helpless as classmates taunted her, teasing her because of the complexion of her skin, full lips, textured hair, and tattered clothing. Like a superhero out of a comic book, or better yet, a heroine, a younger second grader named Honey came to her rescue and defense. Out of nowhere, Honey ran up and started pounding on everyone standing around bullying me.

With the prettiest skin and the longest ponytails that cascaded down her back, Honey said, "You better start standing up and defending yourself because I won't always be around to protect you."

"There are too many of them and they are bigger than me." Deidra cried.

"I hear my parents say, the bigger they are, the harder they fall. The bullying won't stop if you keep letting them treat you this way." Honey replied.

Wiping tears away, Deidra stepped closer to Honey and said, "You're right and I promise, I won't ever let anyone ever bully me again or anybody around me. Thank you!"

Overhearing another slap, Deidra snapped back from her time machine that had taken her back to her childhood and without any further thought, walked up to the young lady crouched down on the floor and said, "Are you alright?"

Before waiting on an answer, Deidra stood and looked around at the bullies and asked, "What's the problem ladies; why don't you leave her alone?"

"You better stay in your lane or get some too." One of the bullies yelled.

The other decided to take a swing, however, Deidra blocked her punch with the palm of her left hand and returned a right uppercut, followed by a throat punch that she never saw coming and rendered her speechless.

The other bully came to defend her cronies honor and tried to choke Deidra with her arm around her neck. Blocking the choke hold by digging her chin into her chest, Deidra flipped the lady over her shoulder and dropped down into her chest, knee first and then started to pound. Deidra pounded her fist straight into her assailant's nose, one punch after another.

Honey had protected her without even knowing her and she was now doing the same for someone else.

Before the guards could make their way to the scene, Maxine stepped in and grabbed Deidra, while Deidra grabbed the wounded inmate.

Inside the cell, Maxine shouted, "What in the hell was that Deidra, is that what happens when you go take showers?"

"Self-defense 101." Deidra replied. "Even the nicest people have their limits. You get tired of being pushed around and abused, you know." Deidra added.

Handing the young lady a tissue to wipe her face, Maxine responded, "Uh, no I don't know and I definitely didn't know Miss Priss Bakery Owner could get down like you just did. We might be kin after all. Behind all of that education you got, I see you kind of hood, niecey."

Taking the tissues, Deidra laughed a bit with Maxine and proceeded to wipe the face of the young woman, she'd just rescued saying, "I'm Deidra and this here is Maxine."

Choking through tears, the young woman said, "My name is Denise; I truly appreciate you for helping me. I mean it's like you came from out of nowhere but I hope this doesn't cause any problems for you."

Explaining the way of the ward, Maxine remarked, "Oh, somehow I think she'll be alright. Besides, I don't think anyone is bold enough to say a word. It doesn't go down like that in here. Deidra probably just won the respect of every woman in here."

Poking her head into the entryway of the cell, Shank peered in saying, "Yo, mad love to you Dee, your name is all over this joint boo."

Maxine opening the cell doors to Shank as Shank came in dapping everyone up, especially Deidra.

Looking over at Denise, Shank expressed, "Girl, God must really like you or something because He sent one of His earth angels to protect you."

In a voice above a whisper, Denise said, "I know I was being beaten and in my heart I was praying to God to help me…and He did."

Sitting on the bed next Denise, Shank asked, "So what are you in here for, what brings you to this palace here doll?"

"The sweetest hello can turn into the ugliest goodbye. The same people who can be candy to our eyes, can be poison to our hearts. Study their ingredients before feeding them to your soul." Denise shared.

Looking around the cell, Maxine said, "Okay…whatever that means."

Belting out another low-spirited response, Denise offered, "The most dangerous things can look like the most beautiful things. Until a man finds himself, he'll ruin every woman he comes across."

Scratching her corn-rowed head, Shank screeched, "Bitch, what is you talking about? I asked you a simple question…what are you in here for and we sitting here waiting to hear the answer in English…plain English."

"I'm here because of a man. A man I should have left years ago but didn't. I'd had enough and tried to burn his ass…is that enough English for you?"

A communal, "Whoa," belted out from the others as they stood looking stunned at Denise.

Patting Denise on the back, Shank replied, "Burning a bitch is definitely something I understand, I understand that English completely. I did the same thing once but what did you do, who did you burn up?"

"Conrad." Denise said through clenched teeth.

"Conrad," all three of the women exclaimed.

Maxine sat down by Denise while trying not to laugh and said, "Baby, who is Conrad and why do you know someone named Conrad?"

Picking up on Maxine's attempt to suppress laughter, Denise smiled and said, "Go ahead you can laugh, I often times find myself asking the same questions. But Conrad is my husband and for the life of me, I've been trying to understand everything that led me to marry him."

Standing up against the wall, Shank said, "You lit your husband up girlfriend?"

Before Denise could answer, Deidre interrupted saying, "Well you know, sometimes the most important life lessons are the ones we end up learning the hard way. Sometimes when it's time to let someone or somethings go and refuse, life has a way of presenting us with no choice but to let go."

In a dismissive wave of the hand, Shank replied, "Oh Deidre, gone somewhere with all that self-help shit, you tried it earlier on me…and I have to admit, it worked. But now, I want to hear all about how baby girl toasted and roasted her man. See, guys will say things like, I wouldn't do you like that but in fact, the whole time, they be doing you like that. That's why I'd rather get me a woman."

Feeling more comfortable, Denise interjected, "I allegedly tried to burn him up, okay ladies, let's keep that in mind, alleged is the word for the day."

"Oh trust me, we are all familiar with that word and Shank please, a relationship with a woman ain't no different. Man or woman, if they ain't shit, then guess what, they ain't shit…either way. You can't give a person blessings they not ready for, even if that blessing is you." Maxine said chiming in.

"True, true…you right Maxine. I wish there was a way to get people appraised to find out their worth, like we should be able to hold people up to a light and see who's real and who's fake, like a twenty-dollar bill." Shank replied.

Speaking up, Denise continued with her story, "I wish that light existed because if it had, I would have learned a long time ago not to be bothered with Conrad. We argued every single day. I felt like I was on a debate team. But you know, it didn't start out like that."

Scratching the back of her neck, Deidra said, "It usually never does."

"When I got pregnant with our first child, that's when the beatings began. Followed by the name calling and belittling. He started to isolate me from my family and friends. Little by little, he stripped me of my dignity and self-worth. Made me feel ugly, worthless, and less than a woman. Gradually, he controlled every part of me, mentally, emotionally, spiritually, and financially…I mean every part. I couldn't tell you the last time I was able to go to church because he didn't believe in God. And of course, you know when he drank and smoked his weed laced with cocaine, it made it a hundred times worse." Denise explained.

"You poor thing." Deidra said.

Snapping back, Denise sharply replied, "Don't do that! There's nothing poor about me."

"I'm sorry Denise; I didn't mean it like that, I was only trying to -." Deidra replied.

Lashing out, Denise scoffed saying, "I know, only trying to what? You think I don't see how y'all are looking at me and judging me with your eyes about how I stayed and let a man control my every move and waking thoughts."

Stepping in, Maxine spoke up to regain control of the cell, "Hey, hold up there 'Lil Miss, you need to calm some of that down. No one in here is judging you, believe that. I don't know a woman in here or out of here who has not at some point in their life been abused in some form or fashion by someone. Abuse comes in many forms and is familiar to all of us 'Lil Miss."

Shank looked up to the ceiling and said, "Maxine, you know, you ain't never lied with that one. It's like you can know a person, five, ten, or twenty years to one day realize you never knew them at all. It's like you learn more about a person at the end of the relationship than in the beginning. I mean, I can definitely relate to what you're saying, you have to come to grips and realize that you get what you accept and you deserve what you tolerate."

"And did you learn all of that from a man or a woman?" Maxine said smiling.

Chapter 7

"I was always told, your home should be the antidote to stress, not the cause of it, but that surely wasn't the case in my home, no sir, it just wasn't." Denise said as she tried to settle down.

Offering a cup of tang from her stash, Maxine said, "Here, drink this."

Looking around at the women in the packed jail cell, Denise continued, "I've learned, what's hardest for a woman isn't losing him. It's forgiving herself for falling in love with his potential, knowing damn well she saw the warning signs and inconsistencies. Women have a bad habit of becoming infatuated with a person's potential. They get so intrigued by what they initially showed them that they start to imagine all the great things that could possibly come from it. Never once stopping to think that sometimes people fail to live up to their potential."

Pouring out every inch of her soul, Denise fell to the ground and cried, the unintentional breakdown was exactly what she needed.

The unlikely group of women assembled formed the wall of support she needed to acknowledge, express, and heal without judgement.

The memories were all too real for Denise, "Every time we'd break up or I'd try to leave, he'd stalk and harass me like crazy. That relationship literally almost drove me insane. I'd always thought to myself, the only way out of that relationship was in a body bag or a straight-jacket. It's true when they say be careful what you think because the power of our thoughts will manifest and spill over into your actions. What we think, we become. I'm a witness." Denise lamented.

Kneeling down to comfort and stroke Denise's elongated ponytail, Deidra pulled her over and placed her head in her lap, "C'mon Denise, let it all out." Deidra expressed.

Having permission to continue on, Denise explained, "A few years ago, I reached my breaking point. I tried to take a couple bottles of pills. But God obviously had other plans. He wouldn't even let me kill myself because I threw up so bad. I knew at that point, I had a problem. I checked myself into a mental institution to try to seek help. After weeks of just pumping me full of meds and keeping me in a zombie state, I figured I would go home and handle my problems like a grown woman. I was ready to stand strong and deal or so I thought. I once heard, you can chain me, you can torture me, you can even destroy this body, but you will never imprison my mind."

Denise's tale of horror and abuse was reminiscent to each of the women occupying the jail cell.

"When I got home, I had about two hundred missed calls and messages from Conrad and people looking for me. On my social media page, he'd even proposed to me and begged me to come back. He'd messaged all of my friends and family looking for me. His voice messages sounded so sincere and he even sang all of my favorite songs on my voicemail. Yeah, you guessed it. I took him back months later AND if that wasn't enough, I married him." Denise confessed.

Exhaling an enormous sigh, "I guess I hoped things would be different this time or at least that's what I wanted to believe and to be honest, things were, but only for a few months." Denise admitted.

"You did what you felt you needed to do at the time baby girl, ain't no shame in that." Shank offered.

"I appreciate that Shank but the truth is, I was ashamed; I was embarrassed that I fell for his same old antics. Not to mention, I felt like I had to fight to make the relationship work because we now had a child together. I wanted my child to have the family I never had growing up." Denise cried.

"Who doesn't want that 'Lil Miss, everybody wants to have a mom and dad, I mean I know I sure did." Maxine said.

Sitting up from Deidra's lap, "Every single time we'd fight after that point, I was even more embarrassed that he would always take to social media. I was always taught that what goes on in your house, stays in your house. They'll bash you with the same mouth they begged with." Denise said angrily.

"You right about that girlfriend." Maxine shouted.

Taking another rest onto Deidra's lap, Denise continued, "I remember this one incident, he had just come back from one of his 'business trips' to Hawaii. I was lying in bed and he was putting away the things in his suitcase. He supposedly pulled out a plastic grocery bag with a white long sleeve collar shirt inside. He called me everything but a child of God. Questioning me about what man left his shirt in HIS house. We fought something awful because I genuinely had no clue where that shirt came from. He threw the bag in my face and stormed out of the house. Only to disappear for the next three days like he did after many fights he would intentionally start with me. I remember picking up the bag because the name looked very unfamiliar. The bag was from something like a Honokikilulu Pharmacy or some weird name. I googled the name, and low and behold, it was a pharmacy in…"

Interjecting, Shank yelled out, "Girl, you better not say Hawaii. Don't you dare say he bought that shirt in Hawaii, don't do it 'Lil Miss, don't do it I say."

Denise raised up to confirm Shank's suspicion, "Girl, I was so upset and felt so betrayed, a receipt fell out of the shirt as I threw down the bag. I wanted to believe so badly he hadn't done this. I mean it's like, the more chances you give someone, the less respect they'll start to have for you."

Standing up to stretch and to reflect, Denise walked over to the jail bars and looked out, "It's funny how they'll begin to ignore the standards that you've set because they know another chance will always be given. They're not afraid to lose you because they know that no matter what, you won't walk away. Sometimes, giving someone a second chance is like giving them an extra bullet because they missed you the first time." Denise said softly.

Surveying the other women in the cell, Deidra said, "You're right Denise, it's like when God shows you someone's true colors over and over again, we should stop trying to paint a different picture. When He sets you free… we should strive to stay free. Too many times, we return to what made us miserable."

Finding and connecting with her voice at the bars that confined her, Denise explained, "It's like they get comfortable with depending on your forgiveness. They get comfortable disrespecting you. Conrad is, was, and will always be… Conrad. Not to mention, guys like him, will have everyone believing their girl is crazy and leave out what they did to make her that way. One thing he didn't realize is that you should never try to mess up someone's life with a lie when yours can be destroyed with the truth."

Walking over to affirm Denise, Deidra beside her new found friend and said, "You know Denise, I never thought about it like that but you're so right."

"I've come to realize, people like that have their own personal demons they're fighting which has nothing to do with you. It's easier to fight you than to deal with the fight they feel on the inside." Maxine exclaimed.

"Take it from me, I know it may be easier said than done but if a relationship doesn't make you a better person, then you're in the wrong one. I won't be one of those people who says you should just leave but as I said, take it from me, everyone has their breaking point. Just remember, there's a difference between giving up and not wanting to take someone's shit anymore…a big difference." Shank chimed in.

Deidra stepped in and offered, "The issue is, there's no real warning when a woman gets fed up. She will keep telling him the last time was the last time, until one Tuesday afternoon, she will just get up and go. When women finally leave, there's almost no turning back. When a strong woman finally walks away, it's not because she's weak or because she no longer wants her man. To put it in the simplest form… she's just tired."

Backing up Deidra's claim, Denise replied, "Tired of the games. Tired of the sleepless nights. Tired of feeling like you're alone and the only one trying. Really and truly, you get tired of him…I know for me, I was just mentally and physically tired. My mind left way before my body did. It's funny because he constantly accused me of cheating but I'm sure it was to justify all of the times I caught him cheating. He listened to everything I'd been through in my life and then turned it around and put me through it again."

"Don't you hate it when men do that? That's the worst kind of man." Shank exclaimed.

Addressing the women with a lighter countenance, "I mean every single time we went through trouble, he would run to social media, or his friends and family. Better yet and even worst, he'd go to MY friends and family, and tear down MY support system. He'd tell a bunch of lies or tell all of my secrets in hopes to have everyone hate me. It's like an animal seeking his prey. It'll do whatever needs to do in order to render that animal defenseless and helpless. Isolate them so to speak. Tear down their support system." Denise shared.

"Some of these men talk like they're in the salon under the hairdryers. But it sounds like, you should have loved yourself with the love you gave to him." Maxine interjected.

"So back to my original statement, never try to mess up someone's life with a lie when yours can be destroyed with the truth, you see if people really knew the person he really was and all of the skeletons in his and his family's closets, they'd be shocked. His good boy image and the family's perfect lives would be destroyed." Denise said.

With a 360° degree roll of her neck, Maxine declared, "If that's the case, why not tell it, why not tell the world who he really is, expose him. Or are you still trying to protect him? The way I see it, he'll be angry, call you a few names and tell anyone who'll listen that you're this and you're that. Only to conveniently forget to mention all of the pain and suffering he put you through. He's a coward, cowards do what he did and is currently doing."

Hitching a ride onto Maxine's bandwagon, Shank exclaimed, "Girly, it's time for you to set the record straight and call him out. People have to pretend you're a bad person so they don't feel bad about the things they did to you."

Reminiscing on her own life, Deidra replied, "When tempted to fight fire with fire, remember the Fire Department uses water.

"What' that supposed to mean?" Denise asked.

Looking around the cell, Deidra addressed each woman, "It's simple. You can't fix yourself by trying to break someone else. You can't block your blessings by trying to teach someone a lesson."

Smacking her teeth, Shank laughed, "Man, Deidra, you always trying to drop some knowledge on somebody, always coming up with some deep stuff. I ain't mad at you though."

Smiling, Deidra looked at Shank and said, "But tell me I'm wrong, look at me and tell me I'm right. Even if you're a minority of one, the truth is the truth. It is better to conquer yourself than to win a thousand battles…that way, the victory is yours. Holding on to anger is like grabbing a hot coal with the intent of throwing it at someone else; you are still the one who'll get burned."

"Now that's both heavy and hot what you just said, niecey." Maxine shouted.

Offering a thumbs up to Maxine, Deidra smiled and said, "Hey, I'm on a roll here, listen up. Always remember no one can hurt you without your permission. Keep in mind, in the end we will remember not the words of our enemies, but the silence of our friends.

Jumping up and down, waving her hands around, Shank exclaimed, "You are on fire girl, what else you got over there?"

Revving up for a climatic finish, Deidra reared back and said, "You know, I've dealt with a man who tried to ruin my life. He then had the nerve to flaunt his next woman, or shall I say, his next victim with our mutual friends. She was just smiling not knowing her life was about to get ruined too. But oh yes, I wanted her to know, you can have my headache. Out of it all, I learned, an eye for an eye only ends up making the whole world blind."

Each of the women listening in the small cell looked at Deidra and said, "Wow."

"That's it, pass the collection plate. I've had my sermon for the week, Deidra has bought forth the word in here today." Shank said jokingly. "Seriously though, it just boils my grits when you're the only person who can see just how evil someone truly is." Shank blurted out.

"Boils your grits, huh Shank?" Maxine said laughing.

Chiming in, Deidra said, "Regardless of what a person says about you, you have to continue to live your life in such a way that when someone says something bad about you… no one will believe them. It's up to all of us to stop playing Checkers in a world full of chess players. I'm sure each of you know, the enemy wants to upset you and get you worked up; and as soon as you lose your cool, they win. However, I do understand we are all human, and a human being can only take so much. Hell, look at me. I'm probably one of the nicest people you will ever meet, but look where I am now."

Walking in Deidra's direction, Maxine laughed and said, "Yeah, but whatever mean or bad act you did to get in here; I bet they earned that shit."

All the ladies joined in a communal laughter.

Feeling somewhat better, Denise said, "I don't mean to pry, but I've told you all my story but I'm curious, why are you ladies here?"

Looking directly at Deidra, Denise asked her specifically, "Deidra, why are you here?"

With all eyes now on Deidra, the spotlight was shining brightly in her direction, "Oh wow, I feel like the elephant in the room." Deidra said trying to ease the tension in the cell.

Chapter 8

Tapping her foot and fidgeting, Denise's voice changed to an octave higher, "So now don't everyone speak at once."

In an effort to deflect, Deidra spoke up and said, "Shank, I'm slightly curious to hear your story and I definitely want to know how you got that name."

"Hell, my name tells my story." Shank affirmed. "You guys know the definition of shank right? Well, I had to shank me a ninja back in the day." Shank revealed.

"So, is that what landed you here?" Deidra asked.

"Yeah, I guess it did." Shank responded.

"Let me guess, a man, right?" Denise chuckled, thinking she was stating the obvious.

"No, a WO-man." Shank replied.

"Whoa, now, I'm really curious to know what happened." Deidra exclaimed.

"I'd been having some serious back pain for a couple of years. The doctors had me on some serious meds that would have me dead to the world when I'd take them. One night, I fell asleep early but this particular night, I forgot to take my medicine. I worked long hours on a pretty physical job so I was really tired, I mean really tired. I'm not sure why I woke up but I remember having a dream about my dead mother that night. We were talking about how much I missed her. It was like she came to speak to me in my dream. I can't remember everything she said to me but I remember her saying she had to go and that my daughter needed me." Shank said, with what appeared to be a tear in her eye.

Leaning in close to Shank, Maxine examined her and said, "Shank, is that a tear, I see?"

"Hush up Maxine, let me finish, young sister here wants to hear my story, so let me tell it. I woke up lost and confused and I thought I heard myself crying. Only it wasn't me. It was coming from another room. I followed the sound to my daughter's room, where I found her balled up in a fetus position naked on her bed." Shank said as she was obviously reliving that night, in her head.

"I pulled her covers up and wrapped her inside of them, as I held her tight and rocked her. I cried out to God to please not let this be what I thought it was. I asked my baby girl what was wrong. My daughter looked at me with this terrible look of fear in her eyes. A look I will never forget. At that very moment, I started to put two and two together. My daughter had gone from being an A student to an F student. At the same time, she'd gone from liking my girlfriend to not wanting to be in her presence." Shank shook her head and clutched her fists as she retold the events of that night.

Lowering her head into her hands, "I didn't want to accept it or believe it." Shank said choking.

"I asked my daughter the unthinkable, I asked her, had my girlfriend touched her. Unable to speak any words, my daughter's eyes told me everything I needed to know. By that time, I heard my girlfriend come back in the house. Most likely from her usual nightly smoke she always took outside. I heard her in the kitchen getting a glass out of the cabinet and as she was pouring herself something to drink, I walked up behind her and asked what did she do to my baby girl." Shank told in detail.

"Do you know this bih had the nerve to tell me, you're high on your meds babe, go back to sleep because you're tripping right now. I look at her and said, I'll ask you one last time, what in the hell have you done to my baby girl?" Shank said as she relived that horrendous night.

Rubbing her speckled cornrows, Shank looked around the room before taking a hard swallow and said, "My girlfriend looked me in my face and said, I taught her what it's like to be with a real woman. Without thinking, I grabbed a knife lying on the counter. My girlfriend broke her glass to try and stab me with its broken glass. At that point, it was either kill or be killed because it was apparent, one of us wasn't going to make it out of that kitchen that night."

Sitting on the proverbial edge of their seats, the women all held their hands to their mouths as they listened to Shank's riveting story.

"My girlfriend started swinging the broken glass at me and sliced the side of my face." Turning to the side for the ladies to see the scar that was left behind many years ago, Shank pointed and said, "See here."

"I've always wondered about that gash in your face Shank but never wanted to pry." Maxine replied.

"To this day, I honestly don't know what came over me but I plunged that knife deep into her chest once or twice. They say, I stabbed her fifty-two times but I only remember the first one." Shank described with a slight smirk.

"Do you remember if you blacked out during the incident, is that how you don't remember stabbing her fifty-two times." Denise said dragging out the fifty-two times.

"Clasping her fingers together, "I'm not sure 'Lil Miss, I can't really say. But I'm almost finished, let me wrap up. I didn't have a lot of money so I ended with a public defender who had less than a couple years of experience. He talked to me like I was just some other ninja they could lock away and I got twenty-five years to life." Shank said while laughing.

"I'm not sure I see the humor in the situation, did I miss the joke or something?" Deidra asked.

"Nah, no joke. I'm laughing because a lot of times people use God as the fall back guy, they always rely on Him in bad situations. But that night was my breaking point with this God of yours. Where was He when my baby girl was being abused, huh? Ain't no telling how she ended up." Shank expressed.

"What do you mean Shank, are you saying you don't know what happened to her?" Denise inquired.

The reality of her nightmare lowered Shank onto the bed, "No, I don't know what's happened to her. She was ten when it happened and I didn't know it but my daughter witnessed me butcher my girlfriend on that cold kitchen floor. She'd been too afraid to speak up for me, she was traumatized. But, imagine my surprise when I found out recently she's paid for me to have a lawyer file an appeal on my behalf. You see ladies, I'm only passing through this paradise temporarily because my case is on appeal. After all of these years, my daughter has apparently broken her silence and they are taking another look at the case. Based on her testimony, they're now saying it may not have been a crime of passion as I was charged years ago." Shank replied.

Jumping up and down and in Shank's face, Deidra smiled and said, "Are you serious Shank? That is wonderful news, I'm so excited for you. All I can say is look at God, won't He do it?"

"There you go with your God again Deidra, I'm cool." Shank said.

Sitting down beside Shank, Deidra said, "Listen to me, here me out for a second Shank. In a way, I understand your resentment towards God, I've been there. However, as I hear your story, all I hear is He's been trying to restore your faith all along. The very same daughter you thought turned her back on you to let you rot from protecting you is now protecting and advocating for you. Redemption is available to all of us Shank."

With a single tear, a slight look of calmness and peace swept over her face. In that moment, Shank was beginning to make peace with God in her own personal way.

Chapter 9

"Domestic Violence sign up available." One of the officers came inside yelling.

Escorting a caramel colored woman with waves of cascading hair, alongside a Caucasian woman, who's wrinkled face indicated she'd been living for a while; the guard continued, "Who wants to sign up? Twenty spots available for this session." Continued the officer.

"What's going on?" Deidra asked while looking in Maxine and Shank's direction.

"Oh, this is a chance to get out of here if you want. But, also these volunteers from the women's shelter come in and speak to us about domestic violence type issues." Maxine explained. "I've been a few times over the years, not too bad. I wouldn't say it helps me, but it's a nice change of scenery. I've never really opened up about my story but a lot of women in there share their stories, give each other help and support. Is that something you'd be interested in Girlfriend. If so, better hurry and sign up." Maxine said.

In a heartbeat, Deidra said she wanted to go. She looked at all the other ladies to see if anyone would go with her. "Aw, come on ladies, let's take a break from this cell for a few. Who's with me?" Deidra asked.

"I'm not feeling too well; I want to just go lie down." Denise replied.

"Maybe this will help you feel a little better and get your mind off of things, come on." Deidra rebutted.

Denise shook her head in agreement. Maxine and Shank followed suit.

"Okay, that's twenty people. We're full for this session." The officer said. "Follow me ladies." The officer said as she led all 20 ladies and two volunteers down a long hall, onto a locked elevator, and into a secluded room on the bottom floor of the jail. Where she directed all of the inmates to have a seat.

"I'm Officer Madisyn Williams and I'm a survivor of Domestic Violence."

"I'm London Taylor and I'm a survivor of DV."

"I'm Mariah Anjali and I'm a survivor of DV."

The two women escorted in along with Officer Williams were all victims of Domestic Violence.

"If at any point, you want to share your story or speak out, feel free to chime in." Officer Williams announced. "Please feel comfortable to speak, we are not here to judge you. We are only here to help, encourage, and empower you all. If we can just reach one of you ladies, then our mission is accomplished." Officer Williams explained.

Sitting down in front of the women inmates, Officer Williams opened up by saying, "I'll go first and start by saying, you are not alone...you're stronger than you realize. Do whatever it takes to leave an abusive situation. You can never get back the years you stay and feel stuck. If you have kids, they are emotionally abused when they witness violence or have to live with a parent who experiences it. It can be really easy to slip into a deep depression trying to act like everything is fine and normal."

Officer Williams was captivating as she pulled back the curtains of her past allowing her to be transparent and authentic in her story.

"For me, my abuse was gradual. I was ashamed and embarrassed. After getting pregnant with our child, the bullying, name calling, controlling, belittling, disrespect, and physical and sexual violence started and escalated. When he drank, it would worsen. When he did drugs, it was worse. I began to distance myself from family and friends. The crazy part was, I always fell for the promises he sang, which sounded like venomous melodies. However, nothing ever changed." Officer Williams admitted.

Sounds of fallen tears and sniffles of familiarity filled the room.

"To him, I couldn't do anything right and he terrorized me for it…this man was pure evil. He threatened to kill anyone who I cared about. He controlled me financially and I was so blind to the fact that I made enough money to stand on my own. This man managed to control my every waking thought. Unfortunately, I dealt with this abuse by taking prescription drugs. I lost all of my self-worth; I believed him when he said I was worthless. T got to the point where I fantasized about escaping through suicide until I actually put those thoughts into action."

Officer Williams had everyone's attention. Everyone listened with a mixture of awe and admiration.

"The authorities were useless, they totally made it worse. It was as if they made him untouchable, no probable cause to ever do anything. I remember one time I'd reached my breaking point and I put him out. He then proceeds to break into my house and stole all of my personal things. When I tell you he stole everything…he stole everything." Officer Williams ended her sentence with a hearty laugh.

Light laughter was heard only because they were waiting on her punch line, no one but her knew the joke.

"You have to excuse me ladies, I'm laughing because, he even stole my sex toys."

Now, everyone in the room was in on the joke and they too shared hearty laughs with Officer Williams.

"Nothing could be done they said. Yep, according to the responding officers, you can't break into a home you haven't been properly evicted from. But listen, where I come from, when your things are put on the street and the locks are changed, that my friend, means you've been evicted." Officer Williams said again with a smirk.

The listening audience also chuckled.

"It didn't help he came from a very well connected family with money. Hell, a restraining order couldn't even save me from him; he was still able to do as he pleased. And to think, he swore to everyone who would listen; I was the crazy one. No one ever questioned why he kept running back to me if I was so crazy? I will say he taught me one thing, I've learned when you see crazy coming, cross the road." Officer Williams exclaimed.

Nearing the end of her testimony, Officer Williams finished stronger than when she began. "Well, long story short, since I didn't like nor understand the law; I vowed to do what I could to change the law. I left my abusive relationship and never looked back. I've been in law enforcement for about ten years now, changing and saving lives, one day at a time. I realized I needed to start living my life so folk wouldn't have to lie at my funeral. It took some time but I knew better so I became better and this is my contribution back to the community." Officer Williams concluded.

Salutes, hugs, and applause surrounded Officer Williams.

"Tough act to follow huh?" Mariah Anjali replied with her sweet angelic voice.

Getting comfortable in her seat in an effort to tell an uncomfortable story, Mariah opened up saying, "My story is very similar to Officer Williams. However, my breaking point came when I woke up submerged in a bathtub full of water. I had no clue what was going on. My last memory was of my husband punching and choking me until I passed out. I woke up underwater and yes, you heard correctly, my husband tried to drown me. As I sat up and looked around, I could piece together what I saw around the bathroom. There were large black garbage bags, rope, duck tape, a chain saw, meat cleaver, and plastic all over the floor." Mariah said as she so bravely held back her tears.

Mariah's quivering lips continued to find strength as she relieved a painful moment in her life. "My husband was passed out on the bedroom floor. He'd apparently overdosed but he had blood pouring from his head. From what I could tell, he'd hit his head on the edge of the table where all of his drugs and needles still sat. I looked up and said, I know that was you God, thank you."

Mariah's story was short yet impactful. It was clear the memory still haunted her.

Up next to round out the trio of testimonies, Londyn stepped up and rubbed Mariah's back in an effort to comfort her before beginning to speak.

"My abuse was more emotional, spiritual, and financial. Just because a person doesn't always put their hands on you, doesn't mean they aren't abusive. Abuse can be in the form of control, blatant disrespect, and hurtful words. Don't ever settle for emotional abuse, thinking it's okay because it's not physical. The day a man raises his hand to hit a woman or opens his mouth to verbally abuse her, he is no longer a man." Londyn confessed.

"For years I tried to leave and he'd get so irate every time I try to go. He reported me for child abuse and neglect in hopes to force me to stay. I experienced a lot of weight lost and a lot of sleepless nights. He was successful in getting me fired from career job by going there and making a scene, making me out to be a liability. I lost everything in the blink of an eye. I know that was an attempt to force me back to him. Sometimes your life has to be completely shaken up, changed, and rearranged to relocate you to the place you were meant to be. Interestingly enough, I've never met a strong person with an easy past." Londyn said.

"Did you find where people would easily say to leave and would never understand why you stayed? Did you experience that." Denise interrupted and asked aloud.

"Yes, yes I did. I ran into that a lot actually, especially from my family." Londyn confirmed. "We try to be loyal, the problem comes in when your loyalty turns into slavery. Trust me, I know exactly how it feels. I know exactly what it feels like to cry in the shower so no one will hear you or to wait until everyone falls asleep so you can fall apart. I know what it's like for everything to just hurt so bad that you just want it all to end." London said.

"When I finally gathered the strength to leave, my ex would use my children to hurt me. Not realizing that an arrow aimed at the heart of me, only lodges in the heart of our children. I became so strong I didn't even want him to look in my direction. I just wanted him to leave me alone and go ruin another woman's life. However, I really didn't want that either. I didn't want another woman to go through what I'd gone through. Which is why I'm here today. You see, God has given me a fervent testimony. Life has given me the experiences I needed in order to awaken me. Lessons kept repeating themselves until I finally got it. Maturity and growth came with experience, not age. Sometimes the most important life lessons are the ones we end up learning the hard way. But every time you are tempted to react in the same old way, ask yourself do you want to be a prisoner of the past or a pioneer of the future? God wants to tell you that everything will be okay. Follow His advice and live your life to the fullest! Don't let anything bring you down and enjoy every single day. You don't have to worry about anything. A happy ending is waiting for you because God is by your side in every life situation. Look at me, look at us and know, you can leave, you can start over and you will alright." Londyn ended.

Chapter 10

Before our intermission, Londyn finished us out with her story. Now that we're back, does anyone want to share their story or have anything they want to talk about?" Officer Williams inquired.

No one spoke up.

Making another attempt, Officer Williams added, "Remember, your past is just a story and once you realize that, it has no power over you. When my children remember their childhood, I want them to remember their mother gave it her all. She worried too much. She failed at times and she did not always get it right but she tried her hardest to teach them about kindness, love, compassion and honesty. Even if she had to learn it from her own mistakes. I want them to know I loved them enough to keep going. Even when things seemed hopeless, even when life knocked me down. I want them to remember me as the woman who always got back up. I'm not a victim, I'm a survivor."

Clearing her throat, one of the inmates, Andrea slowly stood up and said, "Um, hi...I would like to um, hello everyone, I uh...excuse me, I'm sorry."

Everyone in the room showed unwavering support and in unison chimed in saying, "It's okay, take your time."

"I'm not sure where to start but I would like to say something, I'm just so nervous. It's one thing when you think about these things you've endured over and over in your head but it's another thing when you try to speak up and give voice to them." Andrea confessed.

"I know, it can be scary but we're here for you. Telling your story and sharing what happened to you will not only help you but others as well. Go ahead." Officer Williams encouraged.

Lowering her head and fiddling with her hands, Andrea took a pause to think of how deep she wanted to go, she realized she wasn't quite ready to go that far. However, she did say, "You know, it's like what I've noticed is that in each of these situations we've discussed and even in my own situation, these men were nothing but users, leeches…parasites…looking for a host. Sad part is, I know in my case, my parasite drained me of everything. It first started with my mind, he ate away at it and turned it into what he wanted me to think and believe and the truth of the matter is, I don't even know how he was able to do it. Once he had control over my mind, that opened the door to everything else. He held my mind, my heart, my body, everything wrapped all up in his grimy, grungy hands. With everything I tried to give him to help him, he only continued to take away from me. In my mind, the arithmetic didn't add up. If I give all I have to you, you should add to my life not subtract, right?"

The weight of Andrea's admissions toppled her over, overwhelmed by the gravity of what someone else's actions had reduced her life to being incarcerated and she could no longer speak.

Mariah walked over to console and comfort her. The sisterhood they found themselves in was not one by choice but of one of necessity. For each of them understood where others did not or even could not.

"As you can see ladies, domestic violence is not to be taken lightly. In most instances, it never starts out in domestic violence it ends up there but there are signs along the way, I'm sure were there that were overlooked. Sharing your stories can help others to get out before it's too late." Officer Williams admonished.

Deidra raised her hand to speak, as she looked upon the faces of all her newfound friends and family. She had finally gotten up the courage to tell her story but she couldn't help but notice the pale look on Denise's face and the blank stare in her eyes.

"I heard a lady say once, when you stand and share your story in an empowering way, your story will heal you and will heal someone else." Deidra began.

"If someone knows me based on who I was a year ago, they don't know me at all. My growth game has been strong. Allow me to reintroduce myself. My name is Deidra Renee King, and I too, am a survivor of Domestic Violence. Where you start in life does not have to determine where you end. I understood myself only after I destroyed myself and only in the process of fixing myself, did I know who I really was."

Shank, Maxine, and Denise all looked at Deidra with what seemed like question marks on their faces.

"I just want to give some words of encouragement to everyone in here. If God could close the mouth of the lions for Daniel, part the red sea for Moses, raise Lazarus from the dead, make the sun stand still for Joshua, open the prison for Peter, and put a baby in the arms of Sarah. Then He can certainly take care of you. Nothing you are facing today or have been facing is too hard for Him to handle." Deidra continued.

Wrapping up her exhortation, Deidra was interrupted due to the thunderous crash from Denise passing out and falling to the ice-cold floor.

Everyone rushed to her side, Officer Williams administered CPR and suddenly a pool of blood flowed from underneath Denise's body.

Upon the medic's arrival, Deidra pleaded to accompany Denise to the hospital as a show of support. Unfortunately, she was not allowed to leave the jail without prior approval.

Left with no choice, Deidra and the others were escorted back to their dorm by Officer Williams.

Inside Deidra and Maxine's cell, no one knew where to start. Everyone was at a loss for words. No one knew exactly what had just happened but everyone had their own speculations and diagnosis of what could have been going on with Denise.

Before long, lights started to dim and it was time for lights out.

Lying in bed in deep thought, Deidra couldn't help but say a silent prayer for Denise, Shank, and Maxine. She couldn't help but think to herself, you have to pray for your friends and keep them covered. You never know what demons or battles they may be dealing with internally or externally.

A couple of times Deidra tried to fall asleep but found herself waking up several times during the night. At one point, she woke up in a cold sweat, the result of the worst nightmare ever.

Maxine could hear the silent tears coming from her bunk mate. She didn't know whether to go comfort her or to keep silent and let her cope alone.

"Are you still worried about Denise?" Maxine said just above a whisper. "I'm sure she will be fine and back in no time."

"Yes and no." Deidra responded. "I'm thinking about my life… my past life…. my future." Deidra said choking through her words. "My nightmares are uncontrollable." She added.

"What are the nightmares about?"

Unresponsive, Maxine went further.

"Nightmares too much to discuss? That's cool. However, there is something I'd like for us to discuss. We've probably spoken over a thousand words and I feel like I know so much about but at the same time I feel like I don't know you at all. What's your story niecey? You piqued my interest earlier during that session. Not one time did you ever mention in here you were a victim of DV. Does that have anything to do with your nightmares or why you're here?

"I'm not who you think I am Maxine." Deidra confessed.

"Okay, then who are you? Maxine asked suspiciously.

"I'm here because I got tired of my abusive ex, my child's father. I couldn't take it anymore and now I can't believe what I've done." Deidra whispered.

"What's the big secret?" Maxine asked. "Are you here undercover, did you fake your own death to escape your old life, took the insurance money and fled? I mean, I can't see you doing anything too outrageous and I damn sure can't see you killing anyone, let alone a fly. A bully maybe, but not a fly." Maxine laughed.

Chapter 11

During the usual 2:00 a.m. wristband check, Officer Williams stood in the entry way of Deidra and Maxine's cell. Sitting up, they both saw the saddened look in her eyes, they both feared what she would say next.

Sorrow filled her mouth and her eyes, "Denise didn't make it ladies. She'd recently had a miscarriage in her seventh week and never sought medical attention. An infection developed in her cervix which spread to her bloodstream. Yesterday, her tubes ruptured which is what led to her fatality. The doctors did everything they could do but it was already too late." Officer Williams reported.

"Oh my God, you can't be serious...tell me this isn't happening." Deidra cried out.

"I'm sorry to be the one to tell you ladies this. It seems Denise made a very good impression on you. I'm sure you made one helluva impression on her Deidra." Officer Williams said while smiling and nodding her head in approval before exiting the cell.

"Damn, I didn't see this coming. Who knew? Oh my God, I feel sorry for her kids and her family." Maxine professed.

Jumping to her feet, Deidra replied, "I have to get in touch with her family and kids to help see them through these hard times. Make sure they don't need for anything. Wow, this is a really hard pill to swallow."

"A strong woman tries to help everyone else, even when she's fighting her own personal demons; I truly look up to you Deidra" Maxine stated.

Silence fell over the cold dimly lit cell as the two ladies lied back in their beds. Deidra found herself focusing on the cracks in the wall and couldn't help but think about her own situation and began to cry profusely. After what seemed like forever, Maxine got up and sat on the bed with her new-found niece and held her like a mother would their own child.

"There, there my child, get it out of your system. Struggles are required in order to survive in life. In order to stand up, you have to know what falling down is like." Maxine said comforting Deidra.

Wiping her tears away, Deidra expressed to Maxine, "You're so right. Who I was, who I am, and who I will be are three different people. Every next level in life demands a different me to complete it. I will never be the same person two days in a row."

"That's my girl." Maxine said with a nurturing smile.

"You know Maxine, I've fed mouths that talked bad about me. I've wiped tears off of the faces of people who have caused mine. I've picked up people who tried to knock me down. I've done things for people who can do nothing for me in return. The saddest thing about betrayal is that it never comes from your enemies. But through it all, I've never lost myself in the hatred of others. I will always continue to be me because that's just who I am." Deidra said with A look of conviction.

"My name isn't Deidra Renee King."

Caught off guard, Maxine didn't know what to expect next so she listened intensively.

"Maxine, listen to me, the same people who can be candy to our eyes can be poison to your hearts. Study their ingredients before feeding them to your soul." Deidra said.

"Here you go with all that deep and wonderful stuff again, will you please just give me the tea, the lemonade or whatever y'all call it these days. Please just tell me what happened." Maxine chuckled through her words.

"I had to get away. Disappearing and changing my identity was the only way I could escape him. All David had was a rock and he defeated the giant. All I needed was faith in *The Rock* to defeat mine. David's giant was Goliath, Dwight was mine. I should've gotten out of that relationship long ago but for various reasons I didn't. However, I was watching television one day and one of those court shows came on. I remember Judge Toler saying, if you wait until you get your ducks in a row, you will never cross the street. Sometimes you just have to gather up what you've got and make a run for it and I swore she was talking directly to me that day." Deidra replied.

"So what did you do Dei?" Maxine asked.

"You know what Maxine, it all came down to this. I'd been cheated on by Janice, Sharon, and Becky more times than I can count; I'd been abused enough. My kids had been beaten enough, they'd seen too much. In my life, my biggest blessings are those children. However, the biggest mistake is who I had them with. When he beat my son for not eating all of his food, I became THAT mom,

THAT woman. No one and I mean no one was going to hurt my children." Deidra said.

"I feel you on that note. I didn't raise my kinds but trust and believe, if something happened to either one of them..." Maxine professed.

Staring off into space, Deidra replied, "I started thinking about ways to get him out of our lives...should I poison him, try to kill him, should I anonymously report him for his heavy drug usage? I didn't have a clue what I'd do but I know I was not the type of person to do any of those heinous things. I tried to take a slightly higher road since leaving wasn't an option. I knew the only way out of that relationship was death. I learned that sometimes holding on does more damage than letting go."

Serious as a heart attack but said with a laugh, Maxine said, "Yeah, sounds like you needed to get far away from that ole, nights like this, I wish it would rain ass negro."

Taking her voice down to slightly below a whisper, "I started doing my research. I found out how to change my identity and the identity of my kids." Deidra confessed.

With an air of excitement, Maxine asked, "What'd you do? Did you look in the obituary and take one of those people's names?"

"Close." Deidra responded. "There was this girl in grade school who changed my life forever. I am eternally grateful for her. I remember looking her up on social media one day, and saw she had recently been killed in a hit and run accident. In school, everyone called her -."

Before Deidra could say her name, Maxine blurted out, "Ohhh, I know who it is...Honey. Am I right? Am I right?"

"Yes." Deidra said as she held her head in shame. "I saw she was living out of state and I requested a new drivers license from that state, as well as a social security card... the rest is history. I devised a plan to escape. The next time my child's dad left for one of his *business trips*, so did we." Deidra said.

"Wow! That's the shit you see on TV niecey" Maxine said through a big smirk. "You could write a book on your story I bet."

"I plan to." Deidra said.

"What would you name it?"

"I'm leaning towards *Sweet Success* or *Taste Testing*." Deidra replied

Out of curiosity, Maxine said, "Why those names?"

"Because all of the good names like Snapped, Enough, The Perfect Guy, The Burning Bed, and House of Horrors... were all taken."

Both ladies laughed.

"I think those two names can be a clever play on words with my baking success and about relationships in general. Hell, you need to 'taste test' or sample these relationships like you would try samples at a bakery or certain restaurant." Deidra explained.

Reaching in for a playful swat onto Deidra's shoulder, Maxine said, "Gone girl, look at you. I never really thought about like that but you have a point."

Digging deep for renewed strength, Deidra said, "Well, hold on because it gets better. All of my hurt and pain drove me closer to my passion. When people try my treats, it makes them happy. It makes them smile. When they're happy, I'm happy. It can also be compared to the taste testings I've had throughout life. Nothing was ever meant to destroy me, but to make and shape me. Had I not gone through those tests, I would've never stumbled upon my love and passion for baking. God always makes a way, even when I didn't know where I was or where I was going… and especially when my back was against the wall."

"Yeah, I can dig it. Your book will be a big success and bring you lots of money." Maxine predicted.

"Oh Maxine, success isn't about how much money you make, it's about the difference you make in people's lives." Deidra said.

"Well Dei, I don't have much faith in people these days. Everybody that's riding with you ain't riding for you. You let the gas run out and see who helps you push. It's funny how certain people will support you until they realize you might actually make it. That's when the hate kicks in. It's like, you can be the sweetest, juiciest strawberry in the whole entire world and there's still going to be someone who hates strawberries." Maxine added.

Deidra stood close to the bars, holding one of the bars in her tiny, little hands. That night, the darkness seemed to have calmed her. She was free enough to confess her truth to Maxine and it was liberating.

"Prior to changing my life, I used to bake in my home, on the side. However, I always said I would one day step out on faith and bake for a living." Deidra said.

"I don't know much about anything but I do know they say you'll never work a day in your life if you do something you love." Maxine remarked.

"Absolutely and that was my case. I love to bake and I had to come to the realization all of this abuse I was going through was only preparing me, or shall I say, baking me into where I was headed. I can say this now but I'm thankful for every single struggle. Had it not been for those struggles, I never would have found my strength." Deidra replied.

Lying back onto her bunk, Maxine offered, "If an egg is broken by outside force, life ends. If it is broken by inside force, life begins. Great things always begin from inside."

"Well, look at you dropping knowledge Auntie. Too deep for a shallow mind, huh? I must be rubbing off on you." Deidra said with a huge smile on her face.

"Hey, let me ask you something Dei. How did you get the money to start a new life and your businesses?"

"Are you ready for this?" Deidra asked getting settled on the bunk.

"Of course, I want to know." Maxine said.

"Well, my mom married a guy about ten years ago. As far as I could tell, it was the first stable relationship she's ever had. I'd known this guy all my life though. They'd been friends for a really long time. He was at least ten or so years her senior. Come to find out, I never knew until he died, that he was my real father. My mother didn't want to get him in trouble since he was a grown man impregnating a young girl." Deidra said.

Placing one hand over her mouth and the other over her chest, Maxine reasoned, "Do you now think that's the reason the man you thought was your dad didn't accept you?"

Shrugging her shoulders, Deidra replied, "Who knows, I guess it's possible. It's just sometimes adults get so caught up in their issues they forget the feelings of their children."

"I know, we get things mixed up sometimes." Maxine said.

"My stepfather or who was really my father was in a terrible accident driving his company vehicle. His work truck stalled on the highway and he pulled over behind another broken down semi-truck. A second semi-truck, driving carelessly, rammed into the back of him and sandwiched him in between two vehicles. It was so bad, his body was unrecognizable."

Drawing her head back, Maxine exclaimed, "Ouch."

"To answer your question about my finances, my mother and I were named as the beneficiaries on his generous life insurance policy Not to mention, my mother sued and won a sizeable law suit against both trucking companies. Of course, she'd give it all back to have her husband. Having the money only helps you grieve in a bigger house and a fancier car."

"Wow, I'm truly sorry to hear that Dei." Maxine chimed in.

"When I decided I'd had enough of my relationship and wanted to get out, my mom gave me half of the proceeds from the lawsuit plus the money I had from the insurance policy. She told me to run and to never look back. Therefore, I crafted a strategy and planned my and my children's disappearance and for years…it worked."

"So you left, did you have to disconnect from all of your family and friends…from your mother?" Maxine asked.

Lowering her head, Deidra said softly, "Yes and that was the hard part but my mother wanted me and my children to be safe so she knew the day I left that would be our last time seeing each other."

"And was it?" Maxine inquired.

"Unfortunately, it was. She needed plausible deniability when the authorities and my ex came looking for me. However, I always kept in touch with her trustee. The trustee called me recently and gave me the worst news ever. He revealed she was dead…cancer. I didn't even know she was sick. Thing is, I was so overwhelmed, I tried to sneak back into town to pay my respect. I tried to be as conspicuous as possible and as cautious as I could be but someone saw me and contacted my ex." Deidra explained.

"Hey girl, don't stop talking…what happened next?"

"I hurried back home, back here as soon as I could. However, with the thought of me being back, my ex wasn't going to give up, he hired a private investigator who found me. So, on yesterday, I was arrested for kidnapping and endangering my kids and now I'm here."

"Are they going to extradite you back there?" Maxine asked.

"At this point, I'm not sure what's going to happen. If you remember, I thought I was getting out Friday night and I didn't. What's the use in having money if you can't use it to get you out of jail over the weekend, huh?"

"I know right. So, who has your kids, what's going on with your bakeries? Oh my goodness, I'm kind of speechless right now and that doesn't happen often." Maxine said in an attempt to make Deidra laugh a little.

Offering a light-hearted chuckle, Deidra said, "You sound like you still have a lot of speech going on to me. Well, let me see. The answer to your first question, when you reach out to victim's advocates, you end up with a network of advocates, no matter where you are. I guess because of what we all have been through, the advocates really look out for us. In the back of my mind, I thought this day might come so I always had a plan for it, just in case. Some of the advocates I met here when I first moved have become great friends, more like family. My friend, former advocate, Justina and her husband, are taking care of my kids for me while I'm here. My bakeries pretty much run themselves but I happened to be at one of them when I was arrested, my flagship store and the manager there, Erica, a trusted employee knew what to do in case this day ever happened."

"You are one bad mama jama, so, if Deidra King isn't your real name, are you still potentially my niece?"

Rushing over to Maxine's side, Deidra replied, "Of course, that part is still all true and I'll prove it to you once I'm out of here."

"Should I still call you Deidra, like right now, I don't even know what to call you." Maxine admitted.

"Deidra is fine because that's who I am...right now, remember?"

"Man, Dei...I'm blown away right now. I guess you did what you felt like you had to do and I don't think anyone can blame you for that. I mean, I sure don't." Maxine said.

"It's all good. One thing I've learned, man cannot destroy what God has ordained. I used to like the idea of people thinking that I had it all together. Now, I can't wait to tell them how much of a mess I truly was... just to show them what the power of God can really do. Regardless of what this may look like for me now, I've learned God will use your story for His glory. Maybe I'm going through this to be able to help someone else. When God decides to use you, He will baffle your spectators. He doesn't make normal moves. When God moves in your life, no one will be able to deny His presence. I know without a shadow of a doubt God has already won this battle. I can't question Him because things aren't happening based on my timing but I know He is always right on time. Until He opens the next door, I'm going to praise Him in the hallway. If God is making me wait, I need to be prepared to receive more than what I asked for." Deidra testified.

"I hear you but can I please ask you a question? Why are you so damn preachy, where does all of that come from, I mean seriously?" Maxine said laughing.

"Uh, I'll have you know, my grandmother…your mother was preachy. She was one praying, preachy woman and she instilled that in me." Deidra said.

Holding her head down for a minute, Maxine raised her head, "Wow, I wish I could have known her. I wonder if any of those prayers were for me?"

"Oh, I'm sure they were. In fact, I'm certain of it. What are the chances in all of the world, that you and I would end up being in the same jail cell at the same time, huh? Please answer that for me." Deidra asked.

Shrugging her shoulders, Maxine simply said, "I can't."

"Exactly, God does all things well and my dear sweet aunt, I believe this time in here this weekend has been well done. You know what, the best feeling in the world is watching things finally fall into place after having watched them fall apart for so long." Deidra shared.

"Okay, so I have one more question, you said your grandmother was preachy and that's where you got it from, was she philosophical too because you seem to have that trait as well." Maxine said giggling.

Looking over at Maxine, Deidra answered, "Check this out and you tell me, sometimes you have to die a little inside in order to be reborn and rise again as a stronger, wiser version of yourself. You never know how strong you are, until being strong is the only choice you have."

Chapter 12

"Mitchell."

"Grant."

"Young."

"Harper."

The officer stood at the end of the hallway calling names off a sheet. With each called name, the bars would open to the lucky inmate. Deidra stood at her cell praying her name was on the list, she needed her get out of jail card. She was prepared, Maxine had prepped her for the procedure, she was ready to hear her name. With each name called that didn't belong to her made her snap her fingers.

"Calm down, everything's going to be alright." Maxine urged.

"Are you sure? She's halfway down the list and she hasn't said my name yet." Deidra exclaimed.

"That just means she's saving the best for last." Maxine replied. "You know, I'm really going to miss you kid."

"Hey, why do you sound like this is the last time I'm going to see you? I'm getting arraigned today but as soon as that's over, I'll come back and say good-bye and give you my information, all that stuff." Deidra explained.

Shaking her head with a smirk, Maxine said, "Girl, you really don't know how things work around here...but that's a good thing because you don't belong here."

"And you don't either -."

"King."

The cell door slid open.

"It's been nice knowing you Deidra…or whatever your name is. Take care out there and be strong. You're a real inspiration."

Tears welled up in both Deidra and Maxine's eyes. Feeling a tug to go and hug Maxine, the tug of freedom, pulled harder.

"Is King not here? Guard, shut the door." The officer shouted.

Maxine pushed Deidra out the cell, yelling, "Here she is guard."

Deidra stood on the outside of the cell waiting to be shackled and escorted to court, mouthing to Maxine, "I will see again."

Once all of the inmates were in shackles, they were escorted down a long hall, like the chain gang. Everyone approached an elevator, one being operated by an officer behind a bulletproof glass.

"This feels like the green mile." Another inmate whispered to Deidra.

"Quiet…no one is allowed to speak. If I hear another word, you will be escorted back to your cell and you will not appear before the judge this morning." Shouted one of the officers.

A deathly silence fell over the group. Of the ladies in this forlorn group, Deidra couldn't help but notice the inmates with different colored jumpsuits.

"*I wonder what the significance is, why is she wearing red and everyone else is wearing orange?*" Deidra thought to herself.

It wasn't long before she got her answer.

"Stop looking at me, you Bitch. Get your hands from around my neck. I'll kill you, like you killed me last night." Screamed the inmate in red.

Deidra, as well as the rest of the inmates had the most dumbfounded looks on their faces as they failed to see anyone even thinking about touching the inmate in red. It became blatantly clear she was out of her mind. She was yelling at someone or something that only she could see.

"She's been on suicide watch all night." One of the officers whispered to her colleague.

All of a sudden, the most foul smell filled the hallway. The inmate in red peed and pooped all over herself. As crazy as it seemed to the inmates, none of the guards were phased by her behavior. They even had the audacity to escort her into the courtroom and sat her with the rest of the inmates, who were all literally sitting on top of each other in an effort to not sit anywhere near the inmate in red.

Inmates with a lawyer representing them were called before the judge first, followed by inmates with the harshest to least charges.

Unsure of who was to show up for her, Deidra knew someone would, the plan she'd created years ago after her escape, included someone to represent her. Closing her eyes, she tuned out everything surrounding her and uttered a silent prayer to God. "Dear Lord, please give everyone in this courtroom a brand-new start and restore their faith and happiness. Let their best days be ahead of them. Bless the woman deep within each of us, the woman we are all trying to be. Mend our hearts where it is broken and fill every empty space. Lord, erase the fears of our pasts, to create in us a brighter future. Amen."

"Vanessa Washington." The judge called out.

As Deidra stood to her actual name, a well-dressed Hispanic man approached the judge.

With a slight accent, he said, "Good morning Your Honor. My name is Jesus Hernandez and I'm here on behalf of Vanessa Washington, I'm here to represent her."

"Who is this man? Hey, I really don't right now, all I care about is if he can get me out of here." Deidra said to herself.

Unleashing the chains that connected her to the other inmates, Deidra carefully walked up to the front of the courtroom.

The attorney and the judge conversed for what seemed like an eternity, passing papers back and forth between each other.

Jesus Hernandez turned away from the judge and walked over to stand next to Deidra, establishing eye contact with her, he winked.

Unaware nothing short of a miracle was about to happen and unable to wrap her mind around what was going on, Deidra became overwhelmed with emotions.

"Keep it together, this is almost over." Jesus whispered.

"Ms. Washington, do you understand the charges against you?"

"Yes, yes, I, I do, Your Honor."

"How do you plead?"

"Not guilty."

"Ms. Anderson, your plea has been entered and in light of some information I received earlier, your bail has been set, paid, and posted. You are free to leave."

Jesus rushed Deidra to the hallway where every chain that bound her body was broken…she was free.

"Oh my God, I have no idea who you are but I'm glad you're here and I can't thank you enough." Deidra cried.

"Oh no need to thank me, Justina and Tim are very good friends of mine, they've had me on retainer for years. Justina told the kids you were on a business trip, they're waiting for you at your house. Let's go." Jesus replied.

"But wait, I need to go back to my cell." Deidra said.

"Oh no ma'am, that isn't how this works, we've already retrieved your belongs, it's time to go. I can't believe you'd even want to go back there…for anything for that fact. Aren't you glad to be getting out of here?" Jesus asked.

Releasing a heavy sigh, "Well, of course I am, I just feel like I'm leaving something behind."

"I'm sure whatever it is, you can buy another one when you leave here." Jesus replied.

Stopping short of the door, Deidra asked, "Hey, what did you give the judge, what information was he talking about?"

"I'll explain it all to you later but for now, I have strict orders to get you home." Jesus said escorting Deidra out of the courthouse.

Epilogue

"It's almost show time, is everyone ready?" Erica asked.

"Yes, open the doors." Deidra exclaimed.

Standing on the floors of her latest venture, Deidra beamed as patrons filled the store. Expounding on her bakery concept, Deidra opened her first ever café.

Walking over to Deidra, her dearest friend, Justina placed her arm around her shoulders, saying, "You've done it again. The store looks beautiful, you should be really proud of yourself. I know I am."

"Thank you so much Justina, I know one thing, I couldn't have done it without you and Tim, you guys are the best." Deidra said smiling.

"Who would have thought, just a few months ago, you were locked up and charged with kidnapping...your own children no less but locked up." Justina said laughing.

"I know and those were some serious charges...but God." Deidra said solemnly.

"But God, but your mom." Justina replied.

"Yeah but God used my mom. I had no idea she'd surveilled our house all of those years. The proof I felt I could never prove of his abuse, she had it. She locked it up in safekeeping after I disappeared, she didn't want to interfere with that or give him any clue as to where I was."

"I'm sure that had to be hard on her though, knowing you were going through that and couldn't really do anything about it. Not to mention, having to see you and the kids leave. You didn't only leave him but you left her too. She demonstrated selfless love to you and your kids." Justina declared.

Wiping tears, Deidra whispered, "I know. Nothing like a mother's love."

"Hey, dry those tears, the news trucks are here, you have some interviews to do sister." Justina said.

The evidence Deidra's mom had was uncovered by her trustee after her death. It cleared the way for Deidra to stay put with the kids. While she did technically take the children without their father's permission, she didn't have to serve time. In return, she paid it forward and created a non-profit, offering convicted felony woman, a second chance, a chance to earn a culinary or pastry degree and work in her stores.

The head chef of the new café, you guessed it, Maxine.

Deidra, through a team of attorneys, petitioned the courts to remand Maxine into her custody in an effort to rehabilitate her.

Maxine completed culinary school in record time and Deidra made her the Executive chef at her newest restaurant, King's Café.

DNA testing didn't have to prove what they already knew but the proper testing was done and it was confirmed, Maxine was Deidra's aunt and they together were now in search of Maxine's brother.

Walking up towards Deidra, Maxine, and Justina, the first reporter said, "Ms. King, you're doing some amazing things here, life seems to be pretty sweet for you these days. Tell our listeners how you made all of this happen."

Taking a glance around the café, her friends and her family, Deidra took in a deep breath and said, "Life may seem sweet but it takes work...LOTS of work to be able to enjoy eating a piece of my cakes. Life can be hard but I guarantee you, when you find your sweet spot, it will be worth it."

About the Author

Born in Jacksonville, Florida, D. LaShawn is a graduate of Florida Agricultural and Mechanical University and a successful entrepreneur. D. LaShawn is a single mother of two beautiful children.

Though she's gone through life's ups and downs, her life experiences have truly strengthened her and her faith, bringing her much closer to God. With a dream and desire to always become a writer, D. LaShawn has stepped out making her dream into a reality by becoming an author. *Life's A Piece of Cake* is her first novel but it won't be her last. To her, this book is the birth of a beautiful and sweet creation.

To contact her, she can be reached at denenamontgomery@gmail.com

Author's Note

If you or someone you know is experiencing domestic violence, please seek help. There are people waiting and willing to assist you.

Know The Eight Before It's Too Late: Provided by Shalonda Corley

1. **Intensity:** Lying, over the top gestures, insisting early marriage/commitment, bombarding with texts and emails
2. **Jealousy:** Irrational behavior, refusal to let you speak to the opposite sex, demanding to know private details of your life
3. **Control:** Telling you how to dress and behave, showing up uninvited, checking your phone without permission
4. **Isolation:** Insisting you spend time with only them, making you emotionally, physically, and financially dependent upon them
5. **Criticism:** Calling you names, ridiculing your life and trying to brainwash you, claiming they are the only one who cares
6. **Sabotage:** Making you miss work or school, hiding your keys or money, destroying your self-esteem
7. **Blame:** Making you feel guilty and blaming you for their problems, making you responsible for their destructive behavior
8. **Anger:** Overreacting to issues, having outbursts you can't control, threatening to hurt or kill you. Feeling afraid for your life

There's nothing and no one worth you sacrificing yourself, get help today.

Contact the National Domestic Hotline, a 24/7 hotline with trained advocates waiting to support you without judgement.

1.800.799.SAFE (7233)

www.ingramcontent.com/pod-product-compliance
Lightning Source LLC
Chambersburg PA
CBHW030603130626
46552CB00006B/2649